H.K. Belvedere is an author from the United Kingdom. He became interested in writing towards his late twenties but felt he was not quite ready to attempt his own novel. After some deep research and soul-searching, he set about writing his debut novel, *Beyond the Blue Girl*.

Dedicated to all the truth-seekers out there lost in the howling madness. You are not alone.

The masses will wake up sooner or later......777

H.K. Belvedere

BEYOND THE BLUE GIRL

AUSTIN MACAULEY PUBLISHERS™

LONDON · CAMBRIDGE · NEW YORK · SHARJAH

A CIP catalogue record for this title is available from the British Library.

The story, events and words mentioned in this book are solely the author's views.

ISBN 9781528976718 (Paperback)
ISBN 9781528976732 (ePub e-book)

www.austinmacauley.com

First Published (2019)
Austin Macauley Publishers Ltd
25 Canada Square
Canary Wharf
London
E14 5LQ

Synopsis

Katie Brown is a troubled girl from Edinburgh. She suffers horrific abuse from her evil father. She decides one day to leave home for a better life in London but things don't go smoothly for her and she spirals downwards into a life of stripping and drug abuse. After meeting a rich and handsome photographer, Katie feels her life is starting to look brighter but the charming man has other plans for her that involve his psychopathic friend, the Wallpaper Man. She is introduced to the dark world of high society and has her eyes opened to the sick and twisted activities of the elite!

Chapter 1

It was the kind of rain that made the pavements slightly smell. Drizzly rain on a humid April afternoon. Katie Brown, twelve years old from Edinburgh, was walking home from school with her best friend and neighbour, Lucy Smith. On the surface, Katie was a normal and very pretty thirteen-year-old girl but sadly her image did not reflect the reality of her life. Her mother and father were dysfunctional; her dad, Thomas Brown, was a drinker, a bully, a lowlife type but also an alpha male at face value. He was around six feet tall and had wide shoulders. A muscular built man with jet-black hair and dark eyes. He was not very nice to Katie or her mother Margaret. Katie was the only child in the family, she had an older brother but he died during childbirth three years before Katie was born. This tragic event had a big impact on her mother and father and in turn young Katie. Her dad worked a low-paid factory job, which just about made ends meet after he purchased large quantities of booze and cigarettes that he and her mother consumed. They just got by but had little or no excess in life. Christmas and birthdays were not happy occasions, they just tended to aggravate the existing issues and usually ended up in horrific drama and violence, both which a young Katie became desensitised to very early on in her life. They say a child is hardwired into ways of thinking at several key points during childhood. She was hardwired to witness savagery and conflict.

It was around 4 p.m. on a Friday, Katie was glad to be finished with school for the week but knew as it was Friday, her dad would most likely be drinking again. Katie went in through the front door of their council house in an Edinburgh housing estate. Her mother, who was unemployed, was sitting smoking a cigarette in the living room watching TV. She was a very good looking woman in her younger years, pretty blue eyes, blonde hair, cute smile, very slim and petite figure but the effects of alcohol and cigarettes over time have caused her to look worn out, dull, lifeless; no spark in her eyes at all anymore. She was effectively dead already. All the goodness had been sucked out of her soul by her evil husband, who had been physically and mentality abusing her for the past twenty years of their train wreck marriage. The early days of the relationship were not all bad, they had a whirlwind romance to begin with, got married young and started a family together, but the premature death of their first-born child turned everything sour. She could no longer work and was diagnosed with several mental health conditions, she was on several medications and her husband began to drink heavily and would regularly beat her. He became jealous and insecure. One night, he came home extremely drunk and raped her while she was half asleep. She fell pregnant. Nine months later, Katie was born. Her mother thought, being a naïve woman, her husband would somehow change, soften up maybe. He never did, the abuse continued as before, even during the pregnancy and after the birth. Katie was born into a morally broken, horrible home. She was up against the odds from day one. She had little or no chance of a happy life. It's just the way it goes for some people, sadly. She needed a blessing to fall from the sky but in this cold and heartless world, miracles don't just happen. The bad guys usually win.

Her mother said to her, "Right you! Get to your room and get it tidied as your dad is coming home from work!"

Katie sighed but quickly replied, "Yes, Mum," and made her way to her bedroom which was up the stairs. Katie began to tidy her bedroom before her father came home; he always finished work early on a Friday but tended to go to the local pub for several hours before he would return home. It was also the end of the month when her father would be paid, so she knew he would be in a drunken state later on that evening. Her room was never messy (for a teenage girl anyway), but the fear of her father, however, made her take extra care not to leave anything out of place or lying around, she witnessed her dad beating her mum one day for leaving some laundry on the stairs, he left her with a black eye and cracked rib that day. Katie witnessed her mother getting verbally abused and physically abused. She heard her mother also being raped some nights, when things got really bad. At the time, she was too young to understand and assumed her dad was just beating her mother again but as she got older she realised he was forcing sex on her without consent or a care in the world. He knew she would never leave him, he knew he had all the power; he knew he could get away with murder. The Police were never contacted. Nobody outside the house knew anything. They appeared to be a normal happy family to everybody, man went to work, woman looked after the house, young girl went about her business and on the face of it, everything looked just fine. Yet inside, it was the complete opposite.

It was now 7:30 p.m., Katie was lying on top of her bed daydreaming and was made to jump up by a loud thud of the front door being opened and shut in an aggressive manner. She heard her drunk Father shout, "Why the fuck is there rubbish lying on my front path?" He grabbed his wife Margaret by the throat and pinned her to the hallway wall and said, "How many fucking times do I need to tell you to keep my fucking house tidy, you useless fucking cunt!" He slapped Katie's mum around the face a few times and then threw her on to the floor and asked her, "Where is my fucking dinner then?" Katie's mum tried to explain, fighting back tears, as she never knew when he would be home as he never called to inform her. He went into a frenzy and started shouting and spitting in her face: "GET MY FUCKING DINNER MADE NOW, YOU STUPID FUCKING BITCH!" He grabbed her hair and manhandled her to her feet and slapped her a few more times even harder. She broke down and began to cry, saying sorry and begging for him to stop his assault, he let go and she made her way into the kitchen to organise the dinner ASAP. Katie had gradually, over years, bitten her thumbnails during her father's outbursts; she had basically no nails left on her thumbs due to this. A nervous wreck at thirteen years old, her dad had never hit her like he did with her mother but she had a feeling that one day soon he will probably attack her. She was powerless to stop this. If her mother couldn't stand up to him nor leave him then what chance had she got?

Things in the house calmed down momentarily, her Father has had dinner now but was still drinking heavily, her mother had also been drinking to block out the pain of the beating she received earlier. She was still crying slightly sitting on the couch next to her husband. As he sipped his can of lager, he told his wife to, "Stop fucking crying like a baby." She did not reply. Katie was still in her bedroom, alone, speaking to her friends from school on Facebook; she was making plans with her best friend and neighbour Lucy Smith to meet up on Saturday, which was the following day. They wanted to go to the park together and feed the swans who swam in the lake in the middle of the park. They often did this when the weather was nice. It was the only social activity Katie could really do at that point of her life. Her parents were strict and very controlling about whom she spoke to. The only reason she could be friends with Lucy was because her dad knew Lucy's dad and she lived across the street. It was quite ironic how they were so selective about who their daughter socialised with, considering how they behaved at home themselves. However, she was a thirteen-year-old girl and had to obey the rules of her parents for the time being.

Katie heard loud steps coming up the stairs. It was around 9:30 p.m. Her dad entered her bedroom, "How is my favourite daughter doing?" he said to Katie.

She could smell the stale booze and cigarette smoke from his clothing and mouth. As he sat down on her bed next to her and put his arm around her, Katie flinched. She was terrified of her dad even when he was showing affection. He had a twisted and sadistic mind. Sometimes he acted very nice, then in a heartbeat could turn and become a monster.

He said to Katie, "God, you're one beautiful young woman, I hope you don't end up like your hag cunt of a mother, all she does is cause me problems, her cheating, her lies, her not being able to work. Promise me you won't turn out like her, Katie."

"I won't, Dad, I promise," she said nervously.

Her dad got up and touched her cheek slightly before walking out the room. The touch from his cold hands sent shivers down her spine even though he meant it as a loving gesture; his character made it scary. Of course, her mother never cheated on her father, he was just a very insecure, weak man deep down. He had trust issues, anger issues, was very aggressive when angry, he knew women recognise brute strength above all else and used this to his advantage to control her mother. They were scared to death of this man.

Katie pleaded with her mum to leave him several times in private, but her mother was weak, broken, had no money and nowhere to go. She was trapped with this man forever and they both knew it. The only way she could leave his presence was if he killed her in a frenzied attack. Until then, they were stuck with him. He even made her cut all contacts with her family and old friends; she had nobody to turn to in life. When he was not beating or raping her, he would verbally bring her down and belittle her all the time. He never told her he loved her. He never took them out anywhere nice for a romantic meal or even a few drinks at the local pub.

He was a black hole of a man and his family were dragged down with him. The company you keep is vital to your own mood and overall outcome in life. If you are raised by a miserable bully with nothing going for him, chances are you will become one yourself in the future. Most of the time this will be the case and very few (if any) can avoid this. When it comes to friends, you have an element of power in deciding whom you interact with, but when it comes to family, sadly, you cannot be so picky.

Day to day for Katie was not great. She and her mother walked on egg shells everyday hoping to avoid her father losing his temper but the man was miserable, weak and felt inferior to others, so naturally he would create drama and bring others down to make himself feel bigger and more powerful. He felt inadequate, undervalued in life; this combined with his drinking and anger issues was a recipe for disaster. An insecure man is a lethal force if left unchecked or allowed to develop out of control too far. He needed help but, sadly, he was not prepared to seek it and simply took his frustrations in life out on his wife and child. His resentment of them was the driving force behind his sheer hatred. He was a sick, evil, broken man. Katie loved her father at this point but it was only by a thread. This would change in later life. She witnessed her father kill their pet dog one day. A small Jack Russell, the dog had chewed a cupboard door in the kitchen. He battered the poor animal to death with a hammer in front of Katie and her mother and warned them; if they told anybody about this, he would kill them in the same fashion. The dog was swiftly disposed of under the cover of darkness on a cold November evening. The official story was it ran away and got hit by a car on the nearby motorway. Katie loved their little pet doggy more than her parents, they had it since it was a puppy but it was not very well trained due to her parents being drunk most of the time. She was only ten when this happened and sadly it was just another grim chapter in her childhood she eventually just blocked out. Like a lot of other things, she learned quickly that this was just what life was going to be like in her household. It was not a great situation for the young girl to be trapped within. Katie often wondered what life was like for her friends and she would often wish for a better existence. Maybe one day her wish would be granted but at the current moment, it was not going to improve any time soon.

Chapter 2

Katie woke up on Saturday morning actually feeling pretty good for a change. Perhaps it was because she was going to the park with her best friend to feed the swans. It had a little island in the middle of it, which the wildlife used to lay eggs in and use as shelter during the winter months. Katie and Lucy met outside on their street at around twelve o'clock. Lucy was thirteen like Katie, she was slightly taller, had dark brown hair, a pale complexion and nice, gentle green eyes. She was not as pretty as Katie but looked good nonetheless. They were quite close friends; they were always seen with each other from a very young age.

It was a sunny but cool day with a gentle breeze in the fresh spring air, some clouds in the sky overhead but nothing to suggest any major rainfall was due.

Lucy said to Katie, "I think that Luke boy in our class fancies you Katie, he is always hanging around you acting dumb and trying to get your attention."

Katie replied, "Yeah I know but I don't really like him like that, he is cute though."

The pair of them entered the main pathway into the park and it was littered with empty blue plastic bags with beer cans and wine bottles lying around on the side of the pathway. Some of the local troublemakers liked to hang around there at the weekends drinking and fooling around with each other. Lucy had some bread for the swans. She always brought the bread as Katie's kitchen was not very well stocked due to her parents' issues. They had food but only the bare minimum, plus she would not dare to upset her father. The girls approached the lake and saw the swans floating around in a very relaxed manner. Lots of parents with their young children were playing in the swing park just next to the lake. Back in the old days during the summer, they used to have paddled power boats which you could hire out for a few hours. You could choose between either two-man boats or four-man boats, but they no longer operated as the company which managed the boats went into liquidation and left the area.

"Is everything OK at home with you, Katie?" asked Lucy.

Katie paused for a second; nobody had ever asked her that before, "Eh, yeah, Lucy. Sure, why?"

"Just checking," she said. "You know we are like best friends, aren't we Katie? You can tell me anything," she gave Katie a brief cuddle as they broke up bits of the thick white bread to feed the swans, who gleefully lapped up the yeasty treat which the girls had provided for them. There were around seven swans in the lake, all getting a fair share of the bread. The girls dished out the final slice and decided to go and watch the boys playing football across the road in the local playing fields. They were walking along the busy pathway. There were a lot of people out walking their dogs, out on their bikes with their children enjoying the nice spring weather after a very prolonged and harsh winter. The girls were almost at the football pitches where the older boys played at the weekends and some evenings, they could hear them shouting at their teammates as they ran around the pitch competing with each other for victory. There were people watching them from the sidelines, mostly dads watching their sons in action. Katie was thinking about her older brother who died at childbirth, her mum told her that his name would have been Andrew. She was thinking about how Dad missed out on watching him play football while he was growing up. She knew that must have hurt him a lot, *No wonder he is so mean to Mum and me all the time, he is just heartbroken, it's not his fault really*. That's what she used to think but recently Katie was starting to realise his actions were not actually justified, he was starting to act very weird around young Katie as she was getting older and developing into a young woman. Sometimes very strange to the point where it worried Katie quite a bit.

After the girls watched the boys play football, they decided they better start making their way back home. They said goodbye to each other and Lucy went into her house. Katie was walking up her pathway when she heard a banging sound just before entering her front door. She stopped at the door and put her ear up to it so she could hear what was going on. She placed her ear close to the door and could hear muffled voices, her parents were arguing by the sounds of it. Katie took a deep sigh and went through the front door as quietly as she could, slowly opening the door, tip toeing in very gently, closing the door behind her so it did not bang or made a loud noise. She could hear her parents arguing in their bedroom upstairs, she decided to wait downstairs in the living room for the time being. She sat agitated on the couch in the living room; she could hear them upstairs shouting at each other. She knew violence was imminent. Her mother screamed and begged for mercy as her dad began to beat her again. Katie was terrified. For the next hour or so, she listened to her mother being beaten and abused in several vile, cruel, nasty, sadistic and violent ways. Katie switched off her mind during those moments. She would retreat into a shell of herself and her ego would almost honeycomb off into all different personalities to escape her dire real-life situation. She never knew it at the time but she was developing dissociative identity disorder due to the stressful and traumatic events she was experiencing at home with her mother and father. She had lost her true self already – at the tender age of only thirteen.

The day had taken a turn for the worst; Katie's good mood from the morning had been sucked from her in a matter of seconds. The horrible energy and vibe in her house were overwhelming. Like a black bin bag being put over your head. He was beating the living hell out of her mother today. Katie was accustomed to these types of situations but today on this nice, bright Saturday afternoon, it was really bad. They must have had a rather considerable fallout while Katie was out with Lucy at the park earlier. Katie could hear her mother crying and sobbing. The beating had stopped now but her dad was still in a terrible mood. He came swaggering down the stairs very callously. Katie was still sat in the living room, she was really afraid, her heart was racing, something awful was going to happen and she somehow knew it. She had strong instincts and could feel the impending danger that was approaching her rapidly.

Her dad said to her, "You got a problem with what I just done, you little cow?"

Katie froze, her dad grabbed her by the throat and thrusted her against the wall. (She had seen this move done several times before to her mother.) He pinned her to the wall and threatened to beat her if she complained or upset him in anyway at all and she would end up being like her pathetic, weak and cowardly mother. While he had her against the wall, he put his hand down her pants and rubbed her genitals a little bit while he breathed on her neck slowly, Katie was in complete horror and shock, he then stopped and threw her down to the floor and told her to fuck off up to her bedroom. She did. Katie spent the rest of the day (and night) in a very confused state. She cried, wondering why her dad would have done such a thing, why did he touch her genitals. She was really in a very dark, confused place right now. It was a horridly rotten feeling. She felt kind of dirty, used and unclean. Not pure anymore. Katie was only thirteen when this happened; she was not sexually active and far too young to be even considering it.

Her dad was just starting to push the boundaries with his only daughter; he abused her mother for years and got away with it, so he was now starting to corrupt and degrade his young teenage daughter. He knew it was wrong on every level, he knew it was the behaviour of the worst sort of people you could find. But still he could not help himself. He was a demon, consumed by the darkness, such a grievance with life he felt it was justified to mistreat his wife and only daughter. The horrific event when he first touched her private parts was only just the start for Katie. Her wicked cruel and black-hearted father had a lot more in store for her. As did a lot of other like-minded men that she would cross paths with in her life.

Chapter 3

It was 4th of June; Katie had recently turned sixteen. She was growing into a young lady and really blossoming in terms of her appearance. Emotionally, however, she was degenerating; it was hardly a surprise considering her home life and her lunatic of a father. Katie's first love came in the form of a young man named Colin Templeton, he was recently dumped by his first love and he was feeling very vulnerable and swore to himself after the heartbreak that he would never let a woman allow him to feel like that ever again. In effect, he was out for revenge, had a point to prove, a reputation to redeem. This was unfortunate for Katie. Colin was not the best choice of boyfriend, but this is not uncommon with females in general, especially when they are sixteen years of age. Katie's first romance was a fitting reflection of her life up until that point – twisted, hectic, irrational and unstable. Sadly, she did love Colin with all her heart, maybe not as a person but certainly in terms of how he made her feel when she was with him.

Colin was seventeen years old and was considered a bad boy; 'Ned' was the local term sometimes used. He had a car and sold drugs from it all around the estate and surrounding areas. He introduced Katie to cannabis and other more harmful chemicals. He was a scumbag, very tall and slender, had a very toned physique, he carried himself well, he looked as though he could fight (probably better than he could actually fight) but still – image and attitude can carry feeble minds a great distance. He had short light blond hair, always shaved in very close around the sides, lots of tattoos on his neck and body; even his left hand had some bizarre tribal design on it. It must have meant something but it's doubtable

Colin even knew himself! He was not the brightest chap around but – still smart enough to manipulate a young Katie – which he did.

"Let's go for a spin, babe," Colin said to Katie.

He always called her babe, he didn't really mean it. It was his sly sarcastic tone that made it obvious he was not speaking honestly. His voice sounded good to Katie though, he had a deep masculine voice for a young man, unlike his character which was ironically quite shallow. They were out cruising around on the slightly damp roads. It was raining quite heavily that very morning but the weather had cleared up now. Colin had a reasonably fast car, with a very loud exhaust pipe fitted to attract more attention, which was really ignorant considering he drove like a complete idiot and sold illegal substances to his local clientele. He did have some gainful employment at a local garage as an apprentice mechanic but he liked to earn extra income in his spare time to supplement his low weekly wage.

Katie said to Colin, "Where are we off to tonight, sweetie?"

Colin replied, "Need to make a few drop-offs nearby then I'm going to take you up the back roads, somewhere quiet and out the way so we can chill, babe."

"OK, honey," said Katie.

They were sitting at a set of traffic lights, Colin was on his mobile phone arranging a sale of cannabis to a new customer, whom he had made contact with via social media. He organised the drop-off at a local industrial estate. The character he was selling it to was already waiting there for him to deliver. They pulled into the quiet industrial estate at around 7:30 p.m. Colin pulled up next to the new customer's car and opened his window.

"Two score bags here, mate."

He exchanged the two bags of cannabis. 'Score Bag' was the local term used to describe bags of cannabis, which cost twenty pounds per bag. It was not a great deal for the price but that's why the illegal drug market is so lucrative for guys like young Colin.

"Anytime you need some more, give me a mail, bro," said Colin.

They pulled out of the industrial estate and drove away. Colin sparked up a joint as he was driving. He always smoked while he was behind the wheel cutting around. He took a few puffs and passed it to Katie. She hesitated.

"I don't smoke dope, babe," said Katie.

"Shut up and smoke it, shitbag," replied Colin. She reluctantly took the joint from Colin and proceeded to puff away. She had smoked cigarettes before but never a joint. She had about five puffs and coughed a little before passing it back to Colin.

"You've made the roach all soggy, Katie!" he said angrily.

"Sorry, baby," said Katie.

Colin began to smoke the rest of the joint. Katie was beginning to feel as if she was made out of rubber. She felt her head get lighter and started to giggle a little.

"You're high as fuck, aren't you babe?" said Colin with a smirk on his face.

"Yeah I feel pretty weird but it's kind of good he-he..."

Colin had driven them up a country road to a secluded little spot. He planned to have sex with Katie that night. He thought she was a virgin but her dad by that point had already raped her a few times, however, she still told people she was a virgin, obviously. They sat for a little while smoking weed and listening to electronic dance music in Colin's custom CD player, which he installed in his car recently, it was very loud but he had the music turned down quite low on this occasion to avoid being detected by the local authorities.

"Let's sit in the backseat for a while babe, so we can cuddle up and chill."

"OK," said Katie.

They climbed into the backseat of his Vauxhall Astra. It was a two-door car with front seats that moved forward to allow passengers to enter the back seat. They started kissing in the rear of the car. Colin was rubbing Katie's boobs and kissing her more intensely, he was getting aroused at this point and decided to present his erect penis. He pulled it out and ordered Katie to suck it. She had never even done oral sex before but had a rough idea what to do from her past experiences at home. She nervously leaned down and began to suck his manhood, he grabbed her long blonde hair and forced her head down saying, "Suck it fucking harder – as if you fucking mean it, you dirty little cow!" Colin was quite sexually aggressive and dominant.

Katie was a bit nervous still but was starting to relax as she loved Colin and just wanted to please him. He let her suck his penis for a while as he fingered her now wet vagina. He told her he was going to fuck her like a dirty, little whore tonight and make her squeal like a wounded pig. He did use a condom which was surprising for Colin as he was normally quite reckless. Rumour has it, his ex-girlfriend was pregnant at fourteen years old and had an abortion. Colin obviously learned from this and decided to take precautions in the future. He took her outside the car and bent her over his car bonnet.

"I'm going to make sure your hand prints are left on my bonnet tonight, you horny, little slut."

He had hard aggressive sex with her doggy style over the bonnet for a little while before he blew a load into the condom. He pulled her hair while he was pounding her. Katie nearly had an orgasm but Colin stopped just before she came. Katie could feel wave after wave of pleasure coming to an almighty bliss – almost heavenly conclusion but just before she hit the 'void', he decided to call it a day! Her bum cheeks were red raw from Colin spanking them very hard during the session, they stung a little bit but the pain was not too much to endure. Katie liked the pain however and wished he would have spanked her harder – or even with a belt or some type of striking weapon but sadly Colin was not that way inclined at this point in his life. They got back into the car to return to the city.

"I'm going to drop you off now, Katie," said a now relaxed and relieved, his testicles were fully drained, Colin. They headed back to Katie's estate. He dropped her off outside her rundown looking house and then drove away. Not even a kiss or a goodbye. He was done with her for the night – she had served her purpose to him. Katie was a bit upset about his dismissive attitude towards her but at the same time that was Katie's biggest attraction to him. Katie was a very good-looking, young woman. Loads of guys from school and around the local hangouts always showed her attention. Some of them complemented her on her fine looks. She just always, for some unknown reason, preferred the boys who were not quite as gentlemanly towards her. There was something about the rough around the edges, tough looking, cocky and sometimes downright arrogant bastards like Colin that drove her crazy!

She was inveigled with the constant mind games, allured by the perpetual state of uncertainty. She was very submissive in nature so unsurprisingly she was drawn in the direction of the stronger, more macho, no nonsense types. It felt more familiar to Katie if the males in her life were of that nature. Katie went into her house and managed to sneak up the stairs. Her father was not home (most likely out drinking again) and her mother was already in bed crashed out – in a drunken stupor. It was around 10:30 p.m. when she got back. She heard her father come in around an hour later just as she was starting to fall asleep. He never knew about her and Colin – or so she thought. She drifted into a deep sleep regardless.

Chapter 4

"Katie get fucking down here now," said her dad.

She was definitely in trouble for something today, she thought, as she unenthusiastically went down the stairs to see what her father wanted.

"Who the fuck was you with last night until 10:30 p.m.?" said her dad very suspiciously.

"I was out with Lucy, Dad," Katie said unconvincingly – she was quite a good liar usually but her dad was so terrifying, she found it a lot more difficult to fool him.

"Bullshit! You were out with that little toe-rag Templeton, weren't you?" (Somebody her dad worked with had informed him that Katie was seen with Colin driving around the estate.) "And don't fucking lie to me again, you little shit."

Katie quietly said, "Yes, I was with Colin."

Her father slapped her quickly across the face and Katie almost fell over but managed to keep her balance.

"That's it! You're fucking grounded for a week and no Wi-Fi or TV time for you young lady. Now get up to your filthy bedroom and get it cleaned, you little trampy mess! My God you're starting to act more like your mother each and every day. Remember when you used to be a nice young girl? Now you're just another piece of shit lying lowlife whore – you fucking disgust me."

She could smell the nauseating stench of stale booze from his breath even as she walked quickly up the stairs to her bedroom. She entered her room and shut the door. As she proceeded to tidy her bedroom, her father entered the room unannounced after around an hour or so. He burst into the room with a sick twisted look on his face.

"Now I'm going to teach you a lesson for lying to your father."

He ordered her to get on her knees and open her mouth. She was very uptight and apprehensive about it but she learned over time that if she submitted and went along with it, he would be less harsh on her. He then told her he was going to put something in her mouth and she would have to suck it. This was not the first time this had happened, sadly. Her dad had already sexually abused her on a number of occasions before. As always, she was extremely nervous and majorly confused by the whole sordid affair. She was forced to suck his erect penis as he gave her verbal abuse and compared her skills to her mother who he referred to as 'the old washed up and worn out cum-bucket'. It was terribly humiliating and degrading for Katie. He slapped her around the face a good few times also to remind her that he was the one in charge. He ended up bending her over his knee and spanking her bare bottom while making her say, "Sorry for lying to you, Daddy," after each firm strike to the buttocks.

After a while, he got up and put his trousers on and just as he was about to leave her alone, he sat down and put his big arm around her shoulder and said, "I'm only punishing you because I love you and care about you dearly, darling."

He gave her a light kiss on the cheek which sent around ten million shivers down Katie's spine to the point she felt physically sick. He eventually left the room and Katie curled up into her bed – broken, feeling used and violated. Once again, her wicked father had his way with her then had the audacity to suggest it was done for her own good. She knew it was wrong but was completely powerless to stop it. She decided the next day to speak to her mother about it when her father was out. Maybe she could help the situation or at least comfort her.

She was wrong – terribly wrong.

It was a grim and grey Tuesday evening at around 6 p.m. Katie was at home. Her father was out at the pub again so it was just her long-suffering mother and her at home. Katie decided this would be a good time to confer with her mother about the recent events with her Father.

"Mum, I need to speak to you about Dad."

"Oh, here we go," her mother dismissively replied.

Katie went on to say, "He has been acting weird with me lately – making me do things with him. Sexual things."

Her mother's face went blank, she looked down to her right then quickly back up at Katie again. "You're lying, aren't you? Stop trying to get him into trouble with your vile lies Katie! Your father would never do such a thing!"

Katie was stunned. It appeared her mother was prepared to live in denial about what her husband had been doing to her daughter. "You, missy, are turning into a wicked, little, devious liar! Sneaking around with this Colin boy all the time, getting up to God knows what at all hours and now this rubbish about your father! Get out of my fucking sight, you no good trouble maker!"

"I'm not making it up, Mum, he hits me then makes me do dirty stuff with him."

Her mother's face went bright red with anger and frustration. She grabbed Katie by the hair and rag dolled her around the kitchen screaming at her, "Lying, dirty, wee whore – how fucking dare you say that about your dad!"

This was a terrible outcome for Katie. She went to her mother for support, yet all she got was manhandled around the kitchen.

"Me and you are finished, Katie, you're not the girl I gave birth to."

It suddenly dawned on Katie her mother was jealous of her. Since her father began to sexually abuse Katie, he had toned down the level and frequency of times he would abuse her mother. He still beat and sexually abused her, far too often, but not quite as much as previous years. Katie had filled a void in the sick demented man's head and her mother now was almost surplus to requirements. She realised at that very moment that she should have kept her mouth shut to her mother. All it achieved was earning her a beating and now a new conflict with her mother to deal with. Definitely was not a great call. But who was she meant to turn to? She thought despite everything, her mother would understand and somehow be able to help the situation – but no. It only made things at home even worse than before! Katie realised on that day that nobody really cared about her and she was going to be all alone in this hellish situation. She understood now fully, beyond any shadow of a doubt, that she had to get away from this dire environment one way or another. Maybe not today, maybe not this year even, but she knew she had to leave sooner rather than later. And she did.

Chapter 5

"You're going to learn how to read people very quickly in this line of work, babe," said Amanda. Amanda was a prostitute/stripper who worked in the same massage parlour as Katie, now nineteen years old. Amanda was an attractive but plump brunette with huge breasts and nice hazel brown eyes. She had dark skin and very sleek dark hair and was very petite – she also had several tattoos all over her body.

Katie had finally run away from home just after she turned eighteen. Things were not getting better at home and her dad was starting to force her to perform sex acts on him with her mother watching to 'learn some new tricks in their group therapy session' as he put it. She could not take it anymore. She managed to accumulate enough money working at a dirty brothel in Glasgow run by a shady pimp who called himself 'The Owl' (he claimed to be able to see in the dark). Katie was sleeping with 'The Owl' after he met her selling her body on the streets of Glasgow city centre one night. He took her in and let her work in his brothel and while working there, she saved enough money to purchase a one-way train ticket to London. She had no real plan or anywhere to stay but she went during the Notting Hill carnival and thought as there would be a lot of young friendly people on the streets in good spirits, she could maybe meet some friends down there and stay at least for a little while. She was also willing to model, strip and prostitute herself to gain funds in the meantime. She had to escape Scotland regardless. Her traumatic childhood and grim surroundings had worn her out to the point where she just needed a change of scenery far away from home.

Things never went smoothly on her arrival in London. She bounced around off her face on booze and drugs for several months, her good looks ensured she could always obtain male attention and she floated around London from man to man (mostly scumbags) who used and abused her just like her father and previous boyfriends in her past. She ended up homeless at one point for a few weeks near the end of the summer, she slept under a bridge. Luckily, she managed to find work in another brothel and the pimp who ran it allowed her to stay there as she was very attractive and could ensure more profits for his illicit business venture.

Katie then got involved with a half-baked gangster from Shepherd's bush in West London. He sold cocaine and other drugs and was a good bit older than Katie; he was around forty-six when they met in Camden Town at a pub one Sunday evening. She was playing him as he was not very attractive but he had a house she could live in for free rather than the brothel all the time and access to all the drugs she wanted. She stayed with this guy for a few months before getting bored with him. The chap was named Marvin and he was getting a bit too attached to the pretty, younger girl he had managed to scoop up and was constantly declaring his love for Katie. She found this a major turn off and saw him as weak. She ended up robbing him of a few thousand pounds and left him one day while he was lying on his couch drunk after they had a massive argument as he was convinced she was cheating on him with several other men – which of course she was, as she worked in a brothel. She acted like a parasite on Marvin and sucked him of all his emotional energy and resources before she left him mentally shattered, financially ruined and completely heartbroken. Katie at this point never cared – her past experiences had stripped her of most of her empathy and decency – she was out to get as much as she could for herself and at the expense of others, if need be. An attractive female with no empathy or morals is a dangerous creature. But not as dangerous as some super manipulative men as Katie would later find out.

After she left Marvin, she used the funds she stole from him to get herself a private flat in a semi-decent area; she had enough for a deposit and some left over to decorate the flat.

She also had some modelling work lined up in the coming weeks, which was going to be paying a fairly decent amount, plus she was still working at the brothel, her friend Amanda who worked there also was sharing the flat with her which halved the expenses. They got on well enough but tended to be a bad influence on each other and they both consumed lots of drinks and drugs together – this is where most of Katie's income went at the present moment. Straight up her nose. She had a terrible cocaine habit – she justified it by claiming she needed it to cope with her job in the brothel as it gave her confidence along with large amounts of alcohol.

One Tuesday evening, Katie was on her phone to a photographer named Simon, organising a modelling photoshoot. Simon sounded nice and polite, definitely a more respectable figure than she was used to dealing with previously. She travelled to Simon's studio in South London the next day; she was dressed in a green tracksuit as Simon told her his studio had plenty of nice outfits she could change into for the photoshoot. Despite looking a bit common, Katie looked good in the bright green tracksuit, it made her blonde hair stand out more. She really was gorgeous. Her image was her greatest asset. She entered the studio and a very sharply dressed Simon welcomed her in. He had an expensive suit on and looked very handsome; tall, broad shoulders, a very well groomed gentleman with nice styled blond hair.

He said to Katie, "Thanks for coming in a tracksuit; sometimes I wear a tracksuit when I'm at home so I don't need to hide who I really am."

Katie wondered what the hell that meant – it was a very profound statement to say the least. They chatted for a bit before Katie changed into one of the outfits he had in his very well kitted out and furnished studio. She opted for a skimpy female boxers' outfit and some gloves to do a sort of kinky female boxer shoot. She looked really good in the outfit and Simon was very happy with some of the images he captured of her.

He said to her as he was taking several photos from all angles, "You know a good model does a lot more than just look pretty and pose, a good model knows along with the help of the photographer how to create a good image. It's a fine art form Katie, don't let anybody ever tell you otherwise. Also, I need to make a confession."

"What's that," said Katie.

"You have the most beautiful arse I have ever seen on a female – so peachy and plump, its amazing Katie!"

Of course, Katie had been complemented on her rear end before but still she took the ego boosting comment regardless! Can you feed a pretty girl's ego enough?

They spent around four hours taking pictures and chatting away. They got on very well and had good chemistry. Katie was very attracted to Simon and the feeling was mutual. The sexual tension was building up but Simon was very professional and never made a move, even though he knew for a fact Katie was aroused by his presence. He gave off a confident swag and was clearly a man who had his life together. Combined with his good looks, most women would be interested in a guy like Simon. He was a gentleman and he had very good manners and spoke politely, which made him even more appealing – especially in modern times as men like him with good character traits are becoming a lot rarer than before. Katie had never really met a man like him before. He had no ring on his finger so he appeared not to be married and he never mentioned he had a partner or girlfriend. *Maybe he is gay*, Katie thought. Never seemed that way but who knows these days.

They finished up the shoot and Simon told Katie that he would get the images edited and sent over to her. He also gave her £300 for the shoot, which was very nice of him. He was at face value – an honest and upstanding gentleman. They agreed to keep in touch and possibly meet up again for another photoshoot in the future. As they walked out the studio, Simon got into his black BMW M6. It was a very sporty and expensive-looking car. He wished Katie well and drove-off into the busy London traffic. Katie headed towards the train station and made her way back to her flat. The train was packed and it was very warm. A group of teenage boys were stood up all talking loudly to one another. Katie overheard them saying, "Wow check dat ting, fam. She's bare hot, though."

She kind of understood London rude boy slang but she just ignored the silly boys. They were far too immature for her and served no purpose to her at all – other than to boost her ego that little bit more. She could not stop thinking about Simon the whole journey back to her flat. She looked forward to going home to tell Amanda about him. Katie got off the train and walked the short distance home. As she was walking along her street, she noticed this huge scaffolding with several workmen in hi-vis jackets grafting away on the building it was erected around and could hear lots of banging and construction related noises. One of the men catcalled her and said, "Get your rat out, love!" His colleagues all laughed hysterically like silly little school boys in a playground. Katie just ignored them and kept walking. She was used to this sort of attention. It was water off a duck's back to her at this point. She entered her flat and was glad to be home and out of the hot sun outside.

Chapter 6

"Oh my fucking God, he is actually stunning, babe," Katie said to Amanda.

"Yeah, I have to agree he looks well, hot. What age is he, Katie?"

"Not actually sure, maybe between 30 or 40. He is so sexy, I was struggling to keep my eyes off him." Katie was telling her flatmate and work colleague Amanda about Simon, the photographer, she had met earlier that day.

It was around ten p.m. at night. The girls were not working tonight so decided to have a girl's night in. They had lots of drugs and alcohol. After a few glasses of wine with some lines of highly cut cocaine, Amanda said to Katie, "Did I ever tell you about that guy who pissed on me and made me wear a collar and leash?"

Katie gasped slightly – she had done and heard some messed up things but had never went to those extremes or heard of anybody who did. "Eh, no, you never mentioned that. Do go on."

"OK, I was working for this madam in Bolton a few years ago, she had an older husband named Henry; he was a proper slimy, greasy, dirty old man. He was short, fat and ugly and always wore way too much aftershave – but he was very wealthy, he owned several businesses. He always had a thing for me and would get creepy around me and touch me up whenever he was at the brothel. Anyways, I got caught stealing money from the madam one time and she also caught me smoking weed in the building beforehand, which was strictly prohibited. She was really angry and wanted to sack me but I begged and pleaded with her to reconsider. She said OK but only on the condition I would be her husband's no-limit whore for a full weekend while she watched and joined in."

"Fucking hell – what did they make you do," Said Katie.

"Well I was to turn up at their house at 8 p.m. on a Friday evening and was not free to leave until Sunday evening at 8 p.m. So I got ready and made my way over to their house.

"I was really nervous as I approached the house and was shaking a bit walking up their long mono blocked runway, where their two fancy cars were parked up – one black Audi A7 and one White BMW M3. I walked towards the door slowly and rang the doorbell with my very nervous and unsteady hand. After a few seconds, I saw a light coming on through the small window just next to the door. The door opened slowly, the madam greeted me with a very quiet but reassuring grin. 'Come in my dear – make yourself at home and have a fag and I will get you a drink', I was sat in their living room with her and her creepy husband Henry eyeing me up and down while rubbing his penis underneath his trousers – I could tell it was a very large penis due to the size of the bulge. I thought dear God this is going to be brutal that man is a twisted pervert with a huge member – God knows how I'm going to manage this! They gave me a few vodkas and allowed me to smoke a few more cigarettes before I had to submit my body to them and be their personal whore for almost three days. I was really shitting myself but also quite excited at the same time. I knew it was wrong but I had no choice in the matter now!

"The madam and her husband then stood up, the whole atmosphere got a lot more tense and serious in a heartbeat – they told me to strip and place my clothes in the corner of the room in a neat pile. They then ordered me to go on my knees and the madam put a blind fold on me. She told me they were going to treat me like a dirty, little, dishonest pig and make me pay for being a lowlife thief. The blindfold went on tight enough so I could not see a thing. The madam then roared, 'OPEN YOUR FUCKING MOUTH AND STICK YOUR PIG TONGUE OUT, WHORE', which I did straightaway with no hesitation, then I felt a rather hard and large warm object slapping my face – it was Henry's giant manhood! He rammed into my mouth and started fucking my face hard. The madam roared again, 'GET YOUR FUCKING HANDS BEHIND YOUR BACK BEFORE I TIE THEM BEHIND YOUR FUCKING BACK, YOU PIECE OF SHIT SLUT'. Henry then grabbed the back of my head and started really thrusting his giant knob in and out my mouth at rapid speed – making me gag and choke and spurt out all sorts of filthy noises. I must have sounded like an animal and they were treating me like an animal, so it made sense in a perverted and sick way.

"Bluh, bluh, bluh" is the only way I can describe the grotesque sound. He kept fucking my face and I'm not going to lie, my fanny was dripping wet at this point, they were being so mean and dominant over me it was hard not to get turned on! I felt myself puke up a little bit, 'Oh-uh said the madam, somebody needs to clean up their fucking mess!' Yes, they really made me lick my own vomit from Henry's huge penis – it was absolute vile but I can't lie it was making me even more horny! He stopped fucking my face for a while and let me breath normally again for a moment while one of them began to start slapping my tits very hard and giving me more verbal abuse, 'dirty, little, thieving, lowlife, pig whore, how fucking dare you steal money from us, after all we have fucking done for you! LIE ON THE FUCKING FLOOR ON YOUR BACK AND STICK YOUR TONGUE OUT' – I lied down on the floor with my tongue hanging out – still soaking wet of course – the madam said, 'now you're going to lick whatever I put on your tongue', I said OK. Madam delivered a huge slap to the tit, 'OK what? Address me as mistress and my husband as master – understood piggy?' 'Yes, Mistress', I then felt something coming down towards my tongue. I was not sure what it was at first then I got a whiff of what can only be described as shit. It was an arsehole – it was Henry's dirty, sweaty, man arsehole. 'Get your fucking tongue in there, you filthy pig,' said Henry. Yes, Master, I replied as I started to tongue fuck his anus. I have never licked an arsehole before but I can assure you it tastes – well like an arsehole, funnily enough. He made me lick it for a good while then the madam slapped, kicked and punched my body while giving me horrible degrading verbal abuse – she said they were going to use me as a urinal at some point and make me crawl around like a dog, while I served them food.

She also told me they were going to have friends over and I would have to serve them all dinner and crawl around under the dinner table and suck all their toes and genitals then service them all later at the same time, while I was restrained in their make shift dungeon room. I knew it was going to be a long weekend but I won't pretend that I was not very aroused by the whole filthy experience and I realised my own greed and stupidity landed me here in the first place, so I only had myself to blame. They used me in all sorts of cruel and nasty ways and introduced me to humiliation and pain – two kinky sex methods, which I had never experienced before. It made me realise that normal sex, albeit very good and pleasurable, was just not the same as this – I think some kind of special adrenaline or something is realised during that type of sexual activity, before that I had never been so aroused in my life – it was meant to be a punishment for stealing but I ended up enjoying the whole sordid weekend!

"It was now Saturday morning. I was woken by the madam screaming, 'fuck-pig, get up I'm letting you out for a pee'. Yes, they actually made me crawl out the back garden and urinate like a dog against a tree – you know with one leg up."

"Jesus Christ," said a now visibly shocked Katie as she poured them another glass of wine. "So what did they do to you next?" she asked Amanda.

"Well they took turns fucking me – Henry with his huge cock and the madam with her huge strap-on cock – they both at one point stuck them in my vagina at the same time making me squeal like a rabid dog that had just been hit by a bus! They tried to do the same to my asshole but it was simply too tight! They also made me clean their whole house naked while they kicked, punched and spat on me while giving me more

36

verbal and degrading abuse. It was a profound weekend to say the least.

"Then later on Saturday evening, they had a dinner party and eight of their friends came over – it was four couples one male and one female each,, so eight in total and I was used as a servant to serve them all food drink and then after the meal finished, I had to serve them all orally until they climaxed – they all came in a bowl which had the leftovers of everybody's dinner and desert plus their bodily fluids added in at the end. This was my dinner, which I was made to eat. Then I was chained to a rail in the bathroom and used as a urinal by them all; anytime somebody needed the toilet, they would enter the bathroom and pee on my face and body while giving me verbal abuse – a few of the men even made me suck their semi erect cocks before, during and after they urinated… The very sight of me chained to a rail on my knees was enough to make them erect and excited. Again, it sounds horrific, Katie, but I was really turned on most the time – some of the beatings were not so nice but it felt good not to have any control and just submit 100% to these nasty, dominant, heartless people. Come Sunday evening, I was so drained mentally and physically – I lost count of the amount of times I came and I had bruises and cuts all over me. I took, God knows, how much spunk inside my holes and mouth and I had been pissed on more time than an actual public toilet.

"Before I was allowed to leave, I had to lick the madam and Henry's feet clean – even in between the toes and every single crusty crevice while they laughed like demented hyenas. They were proper twisted, sick and nasty perverts, those two – but like I said earlier, I brought it upon myself by stealing money from them.

"By the time I was allowed to leave I felt used, broken, degraded and full of shame – but at the same time I also felt fucking awesome. There is something very humbling about being humiliated – it's like being brought back down to earth and returned to your true raw form as a human being. I found it a massive release and weight off my shoulders, Katie. You should try it sometime just for the buzz."

"Yeah, it sounds a bit extreme but also fun – I'm not going to pretend Amanda, you have made me a bit wet by just telling me your story. I wonder if Simon would be into all that stuff – I would love for him to tie me up and have his way with me!"

Amanda never knew of Katie's past with her father. Of course, it was not as extreme as what had happened to Amanda with the madam and her husband but she did already have a taste of what it's like to be used and humiliated in a sexual way from her father from a very young age. But she knew if she were to do again with somebody who she was attracted to and it was consensually, she may well be able to enjoy it as much as Amanda did. Once Amanda had finished the story the two of them enjoyed some more drinks and of course, some cocaine. Katie was talking about Simon obsessively and it was clear she had taken a serious liking to him. They ended up steaming drunk and dancing around to cheesy pop music. They played the classic 'Girls just want to have fun' by Cyndi Lauper several times a little too loud to the point the neighbour below them had to bang on his ceiling a few times until they turned it down before crashing out in a drunken heap in their beds. It was a fun night for Katie. She enjoyed listening to Amanda's filthy stories and it made her little mind work overtime as she fell into a chemical induced sleep.

Chapter 7

The wind was howling outside on a cold September morning in London. Katie could hear it as she was trying to sleep after waking up very early in the morning, around three o'clock to be precise. She had been having a terrible dream during the night about her father and other horrible men she had encountered in her turbulent life. In the dream, her dad was just sat on a chair looking at her and he was crying tears of blood in a great state of distress. He never mentioned what he was so upset about in the dream but it was a very vivid and profound dream and it left Katie shook up when she was abruptly awakened by the noise outside from the wind.

She was in a cold sweat – the bizarre dream had left her in a weird state and unable to go back to sleep but she was just glad it was a dream and not real life! Everybody gets those dreams from time to time – some call them nightmares but that's just a matter of perception. Katie decided she was not going to be able to fall back asleep anytime soon so she decided to get out of bed and have a cigarette for the time being. She rolled out of her not quite double bed; it was more like a single bed and a half rather than a double bed. She made her way over to her brown-coloured chest of drawers, which had a semi grubby mirror on top of it and she grabbed her packet of smokes and shiny pink deposable lighter. She put a smoke into her mouth and sparked the bright pink lighter. She sucked on the cigarette as the flame ignited the tobacco and she could hear the cocktail of chemicals burn away slowly as she inhaled the thick, noxious smoke deep into her once pink and healthy, young lungs. She slowly exhaled the smoke and then in the distance, she could hear some drunken men shouting. She pulled her slightly yellow nicotine stained white curtains back and could now see two men having a heated drunken argument on the street below her flat. It was a four-story tenement type flat, you know the red sandstone ones you often see in British towns and cities, probably built around the early 1900s and it had the high ceilings inside of it, which made it seem like a bigger flat when you were inside. It was decent enough for Katie but the interior could have done with some upgrades but it was warm enough most of the time and semi clean – clean enough for a dirty and corrupted girl!

The two men were really starting to get aggressive with one another, Katie could now hear them clearly, "Listen you fucking mug, I know you fancy my missus and I know you fucking tried it on with her at mincer's party last weekend, you fucking wanker! You're lucky I don't cut you open right now, you cunt."

The other chap replied, "Shut up, you fucking idiot. I never went near your fucking bird, now pipe down and jog on, you worst cunt!"

The two men began to trade blows – it was not exactly a professional boxing match but they were really trying to knock the living daylights out of each other. Katie stood at the window smoking her cigarette while watching. She felt sorry for them but couldn't help and had a little chuckle to herself at the comical events that were unfolding. She was used to seeing violence at home and around her council estate, where she grew up, so it was not a huge shock for her to see two drunken men fighting each other at three-thirty in the morning after a few drinks too many.

The fight continued for a few moments and one of the men began to spew up – his friend backed off and said, "Fucking hell, Pongo, you're spewing blood – or is it those cheeky vimtos you had at the boozer last night, you fucking poof? Ahahah!" He started laughing at his mate, the smell of the vomit must have hit his delicate stomach also and he began to spew up like the possessed girl from the exorcist – projectile vomit while making very loud and grotesque sounds. Katie was now struggling not to laugh really hard – she ended up getting her phone out and recording the whole drunken episode – she said to herself, "This is way too good to miss," and managed to capture pictures and video footage of them both leaning against the flat walls spewing their guts up after kicking and punching the shit out of each other.

Just as they started to recover from the vomiting ordeal, a police car pulled up, somebody must have heard the commotion and phoned them. The two idiots were arrested and thrown into the back of the car and the diesel-powered engine buzzed off away into the vast concrete jungle of London.

Katie was now making herself a coffee wondering what the hell she just witnessed as she watched the footage back on her phone whilst laughing away to herself. She posted the footage on Snapchat, Facebook, Twitter and Instagram and reckoned she will get a great response from her friends online once they saw the video.

About three or four hours passed; Katie had not been doing much apart from drinking coffee and smoking cigarettes throughout the early morning. She checked her mobile phone to see the reaction from the video she posted earlier of the two drunken clowns fighting then getting arrested. She had several notifications on Facebook and Snapchat but more importantly, she had a text message from Simon the photographer (they only spoke via phone call before), she was pleasantly surprised. The text read, *'Hey Katie, I have been really busy, so sorry for the wait. I should have the pictures from the shoot we did ready by tonight so lookout for an email – Hope you're well, Simon xx'.*

No way did he give me two kisses? Katie was overwhelmed with joy, *Surely that's a good sign, surely that means he likes me? Maybe he is just being nice? Maybe he fancies me? What should I reply back with?* All of a sudden, a simple courteous message became a whirlwind of possibilities and uncontrolled emotions! Katie began to reply, *Keep it simple, keep it professional,* she thought, *don't over-do it, but don't sound ignorant or uninterested. Ok let's do this.*

'Hey Simon, I'm doing fine, thanks very much, no rush, hope you're good.' How many kisses shall I put? Katie was stuck between one single kiss and two. Kisses on text messages are a very underrated and effectively a psychological mind game that people play on each other, especially males and females who are not friends but not quite an item either, it's a very sly way of letting somebody know how much you like them, without actually saying it. It's a very common method of digital courting that has evolved over the years since the mainstream introduction of mobile phones.

It's a very underhanded procedure and you can really play some twisted mind games doing this, for example, if somebody gives you two kisses at the end of the text message you can reply and only give one kiss, or better still, none. It can cause great confusion amongst men and woman and to be honest, it's so intricate and widely used, it could actually be considered a modern-day art form! Katie decided to keep it simple and use two kisses like Simon did. She was just happy he had shown what appeared to be some kind of advanced level of interest in her. She felt good about herself now, which was rare and looked forward to seeing the edited images from her photoshoot.

It was now 1 p.m. and Katie decided to go for a shower and head into the hustle and bustle of central London. She was working tonight at the brothel and needed a new outfit, alcohol and drugs. It was a Thursday evening and this was the time of the week that things began to get a lot busier at the brothel as the weekend approached. She also had a job booked for Friday night after her shift in the brothel doing a strip-a-gram show for a stag party in a pub somewhere near Essex, so Katie had a busy day and an even busier weekend to look forward to!

Katie was on the tube heading towards Oxford Circus. As usual it was packed with a very wide variety of people from all different ethnic backgrounds, shapes and sizes. She had to stand up for most of the journey. There was a young lad sitting down just next to where to Katie stood. She thought to herself, *what a selfish wee twat*. But she never said anything. The boy was sat with his head tilted towards his phone; he was glued to whatever he was doing on his phone at the time. He was effectively a zombie, totally unaware of his surroundings. Maybe if he had seen Katie standing there, he would have kindly offered his seat to the pretty young lady, but no, he never even noticed her existence. The sad part is, this scene is all too common in the modern world, youths glued to their mobile phones while out and about. You wonder what people did before these inventions were made available to the public on mass. Katie got off at Oxford Circus and made her way through the ticket barrier and up the escalator. She noticed the signs on the walls that said 'Beware – Pickpockets' and subsequently she noticed a handful of men all patting their back pockets or side pockets – effectively revealing the location of their wallets and or valuable possessions to any potential pickpockets who happened to be in the vicinity. Katie wondered why the hell they even had those signs up. They made no sense at all. Then again, in this cruel and ironic world, what did make sense?

Katie entered a very packed Oxford Street via the Oxford Circus tube station. Her plan was to buy herself some new clothes, then grab some booze and contact her drug dealer who was based in central London. He sometimes delivered to Katie via moped but today he told her he wanted her to collect from a flat he sometimes used in Chalk Farm near Camden Town. This suited Katie as she would be nearby for the day. She wandered around the busy Oxford Street for several hours, entering a very wide variety of different shops along the way. She treated herself to some new, very kinky and revealing outfits, cosmetics and some other random bits and bobs. She had a semi-interesting conversation in New Look with the male store assistant about current affairs and some light-hearted political chat as there was a lot of turmoil in the UK and Europe at the present time in the way of large protests and a general feeling of dissatisfaction. Katie was not what you would consider a highly intelligent girl but she did have a thirst for sacred knowledge and was partial to the odd conspiracy theory or two. She liked to think there was more to life than met the eye, that the powers that controlled the world as we know it, were somehow hiding the truth from the masses. She noticed another girl who worked in the store had an eye of Horus (or all-seeing eye) tattoo on her back and asked her why she decided to obtain such a symbolic image on herself. From that point onwards, they got chatting about how the 'illuminati' families control the world and the people are slowly but surely waking up to the truth. (Katie had briefly researched these subjects when she was younger and still in Edinburgh.) It was a very interesting chat for a routine shopping trip – a lot deeper and more meaningful than the usual small talk and rigmarole of everyday life interactions that people go through each and every day for most of their mundane lives.

Katie had obtained all her shopping and stocked up on booze from an off-licence. It was now time to contact her drug dealer and make her way to his flat to purchase some cocaine for the weekend. She made her way to Chalk Farm via bus. She got off the bus and instantly saw a commotion just a few yards up from the bus stop. A man and a woman were having a very heated argument. They both looked like they were on very strong drugs, maybe heroin or crack cocaine. They were both very pale and skinny and looked very worn out and old and in need of a decent meal or two.

Katie decided to walk past quietly and not get involved. As she was walking past, she heard the man shouting at the woman, "You fucking, dirty, little slag, you sucked his cock, you fucking scrubber! And I know you nicked my last strip of Valium, you fucking greedy cunt – I should kick your fucking head in, you tramp." The woman was visibly off her face on drugs and offered no response. Katie was attracting a lot of violence and drama towards her. It just seemed to follow her around. The energy you put out always comes back to you, somehow. Sadly, Katie never understood this concept yet, therefore, she witnessed a lot of people arguing and fighting on a regular basis.

Katie was slightly nervous and worried for the woman but she just kept walking and was thankful her drug habits were a lot more sophisticated and socially acceptable. She only took Cocaine and smoked cannabis from time to time – she had never tried any harder drugs; despite being offered on several different occasions. She made her way to the block of flats where the drug dealer lived in and hit the buzzer, he quickly spoke via the intercom, "Who's dat?" he asked in his thick Cockney accent.

"It's me Katie – let me in." He buzzed the door open and she made her into the building and proceeded towards the lift. He lived on the top floor. There were a few people awaiting the lift standing outside in the lobby area, there was very strong smell of bleach like you would experience in a hospital. A Muslim woman with the full body covering garments was there with three small male children with her, standing first in the cue for the lift. Katie noticed the woman was not of Asian descent and she was in fact, a white woman like her. She must have married a Muslim man at some point. She thought to herself, *thank God, I'm not married to a Muslim; he would not approve of my lifestyle at all! Then again considering what I get up to, maybe it would not be a bad thing.* There was also a tall white skinny man standing there with one of those silly bikes that fold up for ease of transport, he had it all folded up ready to go into the lift. The lift door finally opened and they all bundled in.

It made a few stops before Katie was left all alone until she reached the nineteenth floor, where the drug dealer lived. She never knew his name; she got his number from a customer at work and he only identified as 'Da Plug'. She knew that was not his real name. It was probably better she never knew his name for all parties involved. Because you can't tell the police somebody's name if you don't know it! She quietly tapped the dealer's front door – he opens very slightly and double-checks it's just Katie (drug dealers are paranoid by nature, par for the course in that line of work). Katie walked into the damp, smelling and poorly decorated and rather horrible looking flat. There were a few undesirable characters sitting on the dealer's worn out looking couch, one of them, a small stocky black male perked up as soon as he saw Katie walking into the room and said, "Alright treacle."

Katie gave him a half-hearted "Hi" in response.

She then sat down and was keen to get on with the deal and make her way home. The dealer said to her, "OK, what you after again, mate, four grams of white, yeah?"

Katie replied, "Yeah, please, man."

She handed over the cash as the dealer got the bag from under his coffee table. Just as he was about to hand it over to her, an associate of the dealer who was stood at the window overlooking the main entrance to the flats said, "Shit man, the feds are down below, lots of them with sniffer dogs, you're getting raided, bro!"

The dealer jumped up and said in a very panicked state, "Fuck man, fuck's sake! Shit, right let's get this gear flushed down the toilet."

Another one of the associates then informed him, "You can't do that these days, bro; the feds lift the outlet pipe cover outside and wait for the gear to come down and catch it floating out, they will have cops around there now – you're fucked, bro."

The dealer replied, "Well that's fucking handy, isn't it?"

Katie's heart started to race, even though she was not technically in trouble but she knew the dealer and his mates would be suspicious of her because she only just turned up and now the police were there to raid his flat, it's been a long day for Katie.

As it turned out, it was a false alarm. Katie later found out the police were raiding another flat in the same block as it was being used as a cannabis growing factory by Chinese immigrants. Katie got her cocaine and headed back home to prepare for the weekend ahead. She was glad that she managed to avoid any issues with the police and the drug dealer and also happy that she had her supplies in place for her busy shifts ahead.

Chapter 8

It was Friday, late evening; Katie usually started work in the brothel around 8 or 9 p.m. She had arranged to be let away at 11:30 p.m. that night so she could attend the stripper-gram at the pub in Essex. The pimp who ran the brothel offered to give her a lift there and back if she was willing to give him a small cut of her earnings from the stag party to cover his fuel and time. He was only doing this because he fancied Katie and loved her Scottish accent. She agreed as it would be much cheaper and easier than getting a black cab or private hire taxi. The Stag party was at a pub named 'The Cross Keys'. The lads involved in the party had a private function room in the back of the pub, set up for the stripper to do the strip-a-gram show for the stag. The lads were tanked up on booze and had been on the lash the whole night, so they were getting quite rowdy and the poor stag had been abused in all sorts of humiliating ways – this is a British tradition at stag parties to abuse the man who is getting married while drinking to excess and doing a pub crawl around the city. It's very common in the UK.

The pimp dropped Katie off outside the pub and she said, "Thanks, if you can come back around 1:30 a.m., I should be done and dusted and will give you £200 for your troubles."

"Cheers, darling, have a good night, love," said the pimp.

He drove off and Katie entered the pub wearing a long trench coat, which was to hide her very revealing outfit underneath. She went over to the busy bar and the barman came across towards Katie and directed her to the function room where the lads were waiting for her. This was routine for Katie, she had done this type of work regularly and could handle herself in front of a large crowd of drunk and horny men but tonight was a very big crowd and a lot of the lads in the party looked pretty big and well built. They may well have been in some kind of sports team, maybe rugby as some of the lads were very muscular and in very good shape.

The stag of the party (man who was getting married) was not however, he was slightly chubby and short and was absolutely blinded drunk. The poor guy could not bite his fingernails if he tried, and he had a mixture of stale booze and what appeared to be some spilled liquid on his white shirt. He was sitting down tied to a chair in the middle of the function room with a black blindfold on. Katie used a fake name for these events, she used the alias 'Ciara' (she liked to create a degree of separation between her real name and her stripper name). She strutted in, whipped off her trench coat to a loud roar from the men and the strip club type party music started.

Ciara entered into her stripper trance mode and started dancing sexually and walking round the room gyrating in front of the men in the group who were sitting in a circle around the stag. One dude, who was heavily tattooed and built like a tank, tried to grab her bum as she squatted in front of him – she quickly turned around and gave him a very sneaky and sly kick to the shin and informed the guy, "Hands off, pal." Ciara was great at crowd control, she learned that men are always going to chance their luck, so she knew if any of them attempted to touch her, she had to quickly remind them that it was against the rules of engagement. She handled herself very well.

She made her way over to the stag and took his blindfold off and gave him a very seductive dance – not that he was really aware of what was going on, the guy was most likely seeing double vision at this point but he appeared to be enjoying himself nonetheless. She gave him a good show and just at the end as she was about to finish up, his eyes opened very wide and he braced up and puked all over himself to a massive roar of laughter from his mates in the party – Katie narrowly avoided any vomit on her but the smell was really disgusting. This was two days in a row now she had witnessed men spewing their guts up under the influence of alcohol.

The stag got carted into the toilet by his now highly amused chums to get cleaned up. Katie got her money from his best man who was organising the event and she had been passed money by most of the lads in the party as she was making her way around the group. She was only there about an hour or two but now had £1000 in her pocket, take away £200 for the transport and she was £800 in profit. Not too bad for a few hours' work.

It was quick money but it was not easy money, these situations took their toll on Katie. She contacted the pimp who said he was on his way back and would be there in thirty minutes, so Katie decided to get a drink while she waited. One of the lads from the party was all over her in the bar, he was quite drunk but kept putting his arm around her and asking her why she did this for money and she could do better with her life.

These types of men were very common to Katie, she came across them all the time; these guys were the men who really never understood female nature very well and wanted to save this woman from a life of stripping and whoring herself for a living. Katie found it extremely patronising and kept trying to push the delusional and desperate idiot away from her. She ended up running out of the pub when the pimp turned up with this clown chasing her outside while shouting, "Ciara, come back, babe; you're beautiful, I will take you to my hotel and look after you, honey!"

She quickly got in the passenger side of the car and said to the pimp, "Drive, drive, drive!"

He drove away very quickly. After a few moments, Katie composed herself briefly then suddenly burst into a flood of tears. This happened quite often with Katie, her lifestyle would get the better of her and she would feel guilty, dirty and quite frankly ashamed of what she was doing for money and would have a breakdown, usually after a strip-a-gram that was intense like the one she just performed at. Sometimes even after a client was done having sex with her at the brothel, she would have a similar type of meltdown. The pimp offered little sympathy; he did like Katie but he had also heard all this before from the other women he had been involved with. He dropped her off back home and even gave her a cuddle to try and comfort her. It had little or no effect.

She went into her flat, feeling very low and depressed. She ended up drinking almost a full bottle of gin with Amanda in the flat afterwards to numb her pain and take her mind off things. She finally crashed out at around 4 in the morning and was seriously drunk. Katie woke up at around 10 a.m. and felt like shit. She had a headache, fearful thoughts, felt sick, felt weak and it was not a good vibe at all. Amanda was already awake and rather chirpy and to be honest, she was probably still drunk – Katie, however, was not and was feeling the horrid side effects of her alcohol abuse.

She said to Amanda, "I'm never drinking again."

She laughed in a high-pitched tone that went straight through Katie's head and literally attacked her brain – she was rough as hell, this was a proper hangover, the worst thing was she was expected to work extra hours at the brothel tonight to make up the hours lost from last night. This was going to be a very long and hard day for her.

She managed to get some light sleep before finally accepting she had to get up and face reality. She went into the bathroom and reluctantly looked deep into the mirror – she looked like a bag of shit to be brutally honest. She was very pale and had huge bags under her eyes, which made her look older and less attractive. Her skin was all dry and tight, she had really overdone it last night with the gin. It was actually very strong gin that a client from the brothel had given to Amanda a few days ago. It was called 'Naval Strength' gin. It was like 58% alcohol, much higher percentage than the standard stuff – if only she had checked last night before drinking so much. Katie had a bath and managed to stomach some toast later on that day. She was feeling maybe fifty percent back to normal again but still very hungover. She considered not going into work tonight but never wanted to let down the pimp, as he was good to her for the most part and had done her a favour yesterday. It was around 8 p.m. that she decided to have some wine and a few lines of cocaine to perk her up before she called a taxi to take her to the brothel to start another shift.

She arrived at the brothel at around eight-thirty p.m. She entered through the shabby side entrance to the building, which was just off a busy street. It was handy for clients but also well hidden to avoid detection from the police. As soon as she entered the building, she heard a commotion and saw the pimp and some guy she had never seen before rolling around the floor knocking lumps out of each other. One of the girls who worked there had been seeing the pimp behind her boyfriend's back and he found out and went berserk, drove to the brothel and confronted the pimp, which ended up in a fight between them. A couple of knuckle draggers who worked at the place as bouncers ran over and man handled the guy off the pimp and dragged him out a fire exit and slammed the door shut behind them as they went outside. Katie could not see but she could clearly hear the guy taking a brutal beating from the heavies, big mistake coming in there causing trouble, the pimp and his henchmen did not mess around with rowdy clients or anybody who was there at all, any kind of carry on or trouble, the client would be dealt with in a very ruthless and cruel manner – after all, it was an illegal brothel and these guys did not play by the rules. You always got the occasional idiot who would start trouble but for the most part, it was safe for the girls to work in without fear, they knew if any clients stepped out of line, they would receive a fierce beat down and be removed from the premises very quickly.

Katie went into her room where she would have sex with the clients. The guys would go into the reception and wait for one of the staff who worked there to come over to the desk and after the payment was made, they would be allocated their preferred hooker, if she was working that night. There was an old chap called Harold who really liked Katie, he was in his sixties and always paid her a visit. She actually liked Harold as he was a very harmless, lonely, old widower and just wanted some female affection more than anything, most of the time she would cuddle him and do very low-key sexual stuff. He was easily pleased and it was easy money for Katie.

Other men were not quite as nice, some of them were married or had long-term partners but of course, needed a release from a woman they could simply use and leave. They never had any respect for Katie or the other girls and would often belittle them and subject them to verbal abuse during sex, as long it was not loud and as long as they never physically attacked the girls, it was fair game to give them a bit of stick, that was tolerated sadly and they did get some really creepy dudes coming in from time to time. Sometimes Katie would get lucky and it would be a younger, more handsome chap, which was obviously more enjoyable but there is something missing from paid sex compared to natural attraction sex. It had a much more robotic feel to it and it was always on a time limit for a set fee. It was not spontaneous like regular sexual hook-ups, so Katie rarely enjoyed her work. Some guys even reminded her of her sick father, which always opened up old wounds and made her think about her past. This was something she would try to avoid at all costs. It was a fairly quiet night for Katie and she did not mind as she had made a good sum of money the previous night at the pub in Essex and was still feeling hungover and just wanted to get home and chill out.

It got to around midnight and the pimp came in and saw her looking really tired and worn out. He told her to call it a night, handed her the money she was due and sent her on her way. She managed to get a lift back home with another girl, who worked there and had a car. She came home and went straight to bed; she felt better about herself and was looking forward to a good, deep sleep to catch up on what she lost the previous night. Her head hit the pillow and she fell into a very well deserved and much needed rest.

Chapter 9

Sunday morning arrived, Katie woke up slowly at around 10:30 a.m. and she was feeling really refreshed and a lot happier than the previous two nights and was feeling slightly positive and good about herself again.

She jumped out of bed and treated herself to a nice hot shower followed by a warm and wholesome Kenco Columbian flavour coffee, this was her favourite brand and she used to joke with Amanda that it was like liquid cocaine as it was Columbian and very strong. She sipped away slowly on the perky beverage. She then sparked up a cigarette and decided to have a scroll through her phone. There was a text message from Simon that he sent a few hours ago while Katie was asleep. It read, '*Hi Katie, I have those pictures from the shoot all edited and they look fantastic! I was going to email them to you but to be honest I would rather show you in person – I don't suppose you're free at any point today? I'm having a quiet day and have some spare time if you would consider meeting me somewhere in the city? I will treat you to a nice lunch and show you these incredible images – let me know if you can. Thanks, Simon x.*' Only one kiss this time, he was either just being polite or trying to play a game but she was not bothered, she was wondering where Simon had been, he was very aloof with his contact with her, this only made him more attractive to her. She replied, '*Hey that's great, thanks Simon – I can't wait to see them – I'm happy to meet you anytime today as I'm free all day also. x*'

Katie never usually worked Sunday if she had worked the Friday and Saturday nights at the brothel. So it made sense for her to accept the invitation from Simon. Also, she really liked him so there was no way in hell she was going to decline, plus she wanted to see the pictures from their shoot a few weeks ago. Simon arranged to meet her at an upmarket restaurant in Belgravia in central London, one of the most swish and affluent areas in the whole city. It was an Italian place named 'Zafferano'. Simon had asked her to be there around 2 p.m. and that he would be waiting inside for her.

She got herself ready and picked her nicest dress (a stunning red dress) and made sure her appearance was on point as she wanted to look posh and not feel out of place with Simon in this fancy restaurant. Katie had recovered well from her excessive alcohol and drug use over the weekend and was looking almost 10/10 stunning – she was a truly beautiful young lady. She really did turn heads, her image was her most valuable asset and she knew it. Deep down, she was still insecure like most women but on the surface, she was smoking hot and full of confidence and what can only be described as swagger or even a pure natural feminine aura.

She entered the place right on time and the concierge took her over to the table Simon was sitting at. He was wearing a black Gucci turtleneck jumper and looked incredibly handsome and self-assured as she expected.

"Hello Katie, first of all, you look great, sweetheart, that dress is stunning and your hair! Has it been done recently? It looks so smooth and shiny! Wow! Have a seat."

Katie tried her hardest not to blush but she was extremely smitten with his smooth compliments and knew her face was most likely a tint of salmon. "Relax," said Simon followed up by, "I have already ordered us the finest white wine this place has in stock; it's on its way."

Katie sat down and she could smell the aroma of the food from the kitchen and noticed all the people who were also there for lunch. Most of the men were very smartly dressed and the women were also equally as turned out. She noticed a few older women giving her dirty looks, she experienced this a lot, jealousy is a human trait, which is all too common and very difficult to hide, especially with women, such primitive creatures at times, but Katie was well prepared for this, she made a lot of women jealous especially older ladies because their men would always stare at her when she walked past.

The décor inside the place was extremely fancy. It had exposed bricks, which gave it a very rustic look and the tables, chairs and cutlery were made of very high-quality materials. She had never been in such a swanky place in her life and was quite frankly overwhelmed by it but she knew after a few glasses of wine and some food, she would relax and chill out a bit more. They ordered food; they just went for a main lunch course, as it was still rather early. As they were eating, Simon began to talk more and was engaging Katie's full attention – and emotions!

Simon said, "You know something Katie, I rarely meet or interact with girls like you – people who have ran away from a bad situation from home (she told Simon a brief summary of her past during the first meeting when they spent a few hours doing a photoshoot). It's refreshing to meet and work with somebody from a different background. Most women and men, to be honest, that I work with actually tend to be from similar backgrounds to me, well educated and from wealthy families. But I'm glad we met up. Oh yeah! Here are the pictures from the shoot we did." He pulled the images from his briefcase – he had them printed off for her rather than digital form. Katie was very impressed by them.

"Oh my God, Simon," she touched his hand slightly, "These are amazing! Wow! Thank you so much, I can't believe you paid me for these!"

Simon replied, "My pleasure, sweetheart; it was a privilege my dear and I will be honest, I would be happy to work with you again at some point, maybe a different themed shoot or some other stuff I'm also involved with, if possible, we will see how it goes."

Katie wondered what he meant by 'other stuff', it was very vague. But she never questioned him, Simon had a vibe around him that made her just know instinctively that he was a well-connected guy with a lot of good stuff going for him, plenty of money and resources, which of course is what most women find attractive. He only did photography work for fun really, he actually ran a very well known hedge fund in the city of London and also had an asset management company in the city and also acted as an advisor for the senior management of a big bank, he was very wealthy and it showed in his appearance and attitude.

She tried to pluck up the courage to ask him what he meant by 'other stuff' but just as she was going to speak up, the waiter turned up with the lunch. He had jet-black hair and olive oil toned healthy-looking skin. He was the stereotypical Italian looking waiter with a very thick southern Italian accent and he could have been pulled straight from the extra's cast in some mob movie like 'The Godfather' or 'Good-fellas'.

They had lunch and some wine and another brief chat about Simon's business interests and his photography work. He told her he knew the restaurant owner's wife, she was a supermodel from Milan and Simon had been over there and done a photoshoot for her, which was scheduled to be published in the Italia Vogue magazine.

The wine had started to affect Katie; she was feeling merry and giddy and was flirting more with Simon. She was giggling like a schoolgirl every time he said anything even semi-funny, he played it down however, he was used to hot women flirting with him and could handle himself. He had other plans for Katie, which at this point she was unaware of. He may have seemed very nice on the surface but behind the flash cars, suits, good looks and expensive clothing, there was a very dark demon lurking within the depths of his soul.

Simon was a psychopath. He had little or no empathy for others and would do anything to anybody if it served his own secret agenda. He could stab somebody to death and walk away unaffected then sleep like a baby. He was a very dangerous man and he mingled with like-minded characters in his working life and for his jollies at the weekend.

The stuff he was into was not pretty and young naïve Katie had no idea at all what she was letting herself into at this point. She was being led down a very dark path by this handsome gentleman and was in for a very rude awakening in the not too distant future. They finished up their lunch and

Simon, of course, paid the bill. He asked Katie on their way out of the restaurant what she was doing for the rest of the day; she never had plans, so he invited her back to one of his city penthouse suite apartments, which was only a ten-minute drive from the restaurant. She agreed and off they went into the busy roads of central London.

Simon pulled into the underground parking lot beneath the apartment complex where he had the penthouse suite. He told her he was on the sixteenth floor, the very top floor; apartment number 16/1 to be precise.

They went up in the very fast and modern elevator, it only took around fifteen seconds to reach the top floor and it looked very fancy and upmarket. Katie was semi-drunk but still in control of her mind and body. 'Ding-dong', the elevator stopped at the top and the big, shiny, silver doors opened at the same time, the lift speaker system informed them it was "Floor number 16". Simon led the way into the suite.

The place was immaculate from top to bottom and the view was outstanding, you could see the London skyline in all directions for several miles, as the whole wall was made out of very thick-looking, expensive glass. He offered Katie a gin and also made himself one and told her to take a seat on his massive, slightly rounded, leather couch.

He sat directly across from her on a single armchair and said, "Yeah, I do OK in life Katie, I worked hard all my life so it's only logical I enjoy the fruits of one's labour, wouldn't you agree, my dear?"

"Yeah, sure, Simon; you certainly appear to have things in good order. Can I ask you something Simon?"

"Sure, Katie."

"What did you mean earlier when you said about us doing more photoshoots and 'other stuff'?"

Simon smiled slightly and slowly closed his eyes then opened them again even wider than they were before. He had piercing blue eyes; they were very seductive and Katie was mesmerised by them. He stood up and wandered over to the window without saying a word for a brief moment before taking a sip of his gin and saying, "Katie, my dear, people such as me and my kind, we have, shall I say, more peculiar tastes in life. I mean, we are comfortable in life, we have the money in the bank, the businesses, the nice cars, the ability to travel freely and express ourselves however we wish really. The truth is, and I trust you will understand despite coming from a less affluent background, that after a while of being able to do everything you want, you tend to hit a ceiling and become bored and seek out more raw and extreme experiences to fill the void in your life, if you understand what I mean by that. We don't get the same feeling from spending fifty thousand pounds on a weekend that we used to at the start. Sleeping with a beautiful woman is not the same as it once was. We crave power and we crave control over others to fulfil us. You may think this sounds cruel or twisted but in fact, we believe it's a perfectly natural progression and take great pleasure in owning peoples' mind, body and in some cases soul."

Katie was slightly taken aback from this, she understood the basic concept of what he was saying but it was still lacking detail, she asked him to expand more. He walked over to her and touched her cheek, this sent shivers down her spine and for a brief moment she thought about her father when he used to do the same thing in her younger years.

"Katie, my darling, I feel for me to expand, I really must show you what we consider fun. Next Friday evening, I'm going to invite you to a very big country mansion on the outskirts of north London near Watford for a social event me and friends attend regularly; it's a stately home and it's very nice and it's also a private and exclusive party, members only. You can come as my guest and you will gain an insight into what we do. Would you consider joining me?"

"Sure, Simon, sounds fun."

Katie knew she would probably have to work on Friday but she knew if she sweet-talked the pimp and maybe gave him a 'favour' beforehand, she could get the night off. She never wanted to miss this event that Simon spoke so passionately about.

The date was set and Simon agreed to collect her from her flat and take her to the party. They sat for a few hours and chatted away more before Simon told her he had a lot of work-related tasks to take care of and needed to go into his office. He dropped her off at a train station on the way there. Katie made her way home slightly drunk and with a head which could only be described as being full of bumble bees! She was extremely interested in Simon and what he did, as he was so vague and always left a lot to the imagination, she thought about him the whole journey home and most of that day and evening. Katie was being manipulated and was going to witness some events in the very close future that would shock her to the core of her soul! And considering what she went through already in her turbulent life, that was no easy feat!

Chapter 10

The week after could not have been more boring and mundane since Katie had met Simon for Lunch on the Sunday. It was a quiet one for Katie at the brothel and she was actually for some unknown reason not drinking or doing drugs as much. She somehow temporary gained a more sensible and stable head since meeting Simon that day. Maybe he was starting to rub off on her. He had also been in contact more often, which Katie found strange but she was not complaining as she loved chatting to him. Sadly, he was not speaking to her because he cared about her or wanted to have conversations with her, he was simply just putting her into a false sense of security so she would lower her guard more and allow him to really get inside her already damaged mind and gain more control over her. It was very vindictive and borderline evil but people like Simon never cared about that. It was all about him and his own gratification.

Katie and Amanda went out to the shops together on a Thursday afternoon. Katie wanted a new outfit for this event Simon had invited her to, he had informed her to dress smart and transferred her money to buy something really nice. Katie had no issues taking money from men as it was her bread and butter and she of course wanted to look good going to this big fancy mansion with Simon. They were on a busy street in central London and the two of them looked really attractive, most if not all the teenage and adult males would stare at them and some (as boys tend to do) would whistle and try to get their attention. It was pointless, they just brushed it off but they did enjoy the attention and the temporary ego boost.

Katie was feeling really good again and the two of them were in good spirits that day. Amanda had started seeing a new boyfriend and he was very understanding about her choice of employment so she was feeling loved up and Katie was also becoming a bit obsessed and loved up with Simon, so they had a great vibe and chatted while they shopped. It was sunny and dry, which was an added bonus.

Katie was chatting to Amanda, "I can't wait till tomorrow, babe. He is taking me to a big mansion to some private party with his rich friends, it should be good but I'm still a bit nervous."

"Don't worry, sweetie," said Amanda, "You will be fine, just relax and go with the flow, you never know maybe he will take you home and fuck you senseless this time."

Katie smiled like a demented cat, "That would be so good, I bet he is great in bed, has such a nice body on him, I think he has a six pack but I'm not sure, hopefully I'll find out soon."

Amanda replied, "You do know most of those rich, older guys are into proper nasty sex, don't you?"

"Like what?" asked Katie.

"I bet you he is into S&M, rough sex, using whips, belts, all that kind of stuff, humiliation etc., you know, like that madam and her husband who used me for a weekend with their friends, do you remember me telling you about that?"

Katie burst out laughing. "How could I fucking forget that story! That was really extreme shit Amanda. Hey, I'm not saying I would not be up for trying similar stuff, but Simon seems a bit too clean cut for that, but he has said some things that would maybe suggest he could be into that stuff."

Katie really was naïve; she had no clue how extreme and hard-core Simon could be with his 'hobbies'. She was in for a huge shock.

Amanda said, "I bet he ends up being into all that mad shit."

"Maybe," said Katie as she smiles gleefully like a little girl. "To be honest, Amanda, Simon could do anything to me, I don't think I could resist or even want to!"

"Aww you really like him, don't you? I really like Jake also (Jake was her new boyfriend). He is so hot and good in bed; he actually treats me like an animal. I can't stop thinking about him, he never really talks much either, which to start with I never found nice but now I just can't seem to work him out, he keeps it cool. I'm going to stay over at his house at the weekend, I was going to ask him to come out and have a drink with us but you now have other plans."

"Yeah, maybe another night babe," said Katie.

They got all the shopping they required and were making their way home when all of a sudden, the skies just opened up and it starting lashing down with rain.

"Fucking hell man!" said Amanda. "Where the actual fuck did that come from? My bloody hair will be fucked!" It was the kind of rain that actually bounced off your head and had you soaked from top to bottom.

They managed to make their way to the train station and get on the train before it started coming down really bad. As they were sitting on the train, an almighty rumble crackled from the sky above, it was thunder and lightning. Maybe it was symbolic of the danger that was impending for Katie but she never took much notice. They got off the train and made their way home. Katie had agreed to work later on the Thursday and the pimp would give her Friday off, if she gave him a blowjob. A small price to pay, he always ejaculated quickly because he really fancied her so she was not that bothered about it.

It was actually quite a busy night at the brothel; Katie managed to go outside for a cigarette break when there were no clients in. She chatted to one of the bouncer guys who worked there, Big Douglas was his name, he was a nice hearted big chap but if you crossed him, he would rip your head off your shoulders. Big Douglas and Katie got along well and she told him about her plans for the following night with Simon.

"Watford, you say?" said Big Douglas.

"Yeah, she said North London/Watford area."

Douglas replied, "It's really funny you mention that, Katie. When I was younger, I did private security for really rich people who went to some sort of event there. I would drive them up there and wait outside for them to come back out when they were finished up. They stayed in there from like 11 p.m. till sometimes around five in the morning. They never told us what they were doing inside but I remember one of the lads who worked with me at the time said he heard they had some sort of competition where really good looking women who had been kidnapped from eastern Europe would fight each other to the death and the rich people who attended would place bets on the fights. I always thought it was bullshit personally, sounds a bit farfetched to me but be careful nonetheless, Katie. Rich people can be very dangerous if you upset them."

Katie paused for a minute and slowly smoked her cigarette right down to the butt. She remembered what Simon had been saying to her at his penthouse that day and began to wonder what the hell she was actually signing up for. She gave it a second thought and decided she was going to attend regardless. She never wanted to let Simon down but the conversation with Big Douglas did actually spook her slightly but she was already committed to the event so had to attend. This was her warning and she chose to ignore it; she froze because her instincts kicked in and she knew deep down this was most likely a bad idea. (Ignore your instincts at your peril!)

Katie found this out the hard way. She had two more clients in before she was able to leave and make her way home. She usually had a drink when she was finished to numb the pain of being a prostitute for a living but tonight she decided she wanted to be sober and remain fresh for tomorrow evening's event with the mysterious Simon.

Chapter 11

It was a dark Friday evening in the huge, metropolitan, urban jungle named London. Katie was sitting, all ready to go with Simon to the event. She was kitted out in a really fancy cocktail dress and looked like a very high-class woman tonight. She had her hair done up all pretty in a beehive type style, like those American beauty queens you would see in old movies and TV shows. Tonight, any man would be proud to take her out on a date.

She was being collected from her flat at 8 p.m. sharp. It was 7 p.m. just now and she was feeling a combination of nerves and excitement and was eager to get on with the proceedings.

She sparked a cigarette while she waited and slowly inhaled and exhaled the smoke while gazing out her bedroom window. 8 p.m. arrived and her phone rang, Simon said very abruptly, "Outside now." She quickly got her stuff together and made her way to his car.

They sped off towards North London and Simon seemed to be in a good chirpy mood.

He turned around to Katie, while he was cruising along the motorway and said very calmly, "Tonight, my dear, you're going to experience the fruits of high society; you're going to see what having fun is all about, darling. I understand you will be nervous but please try and relax; we are just having some relaxing downtime."

Katie sat quietly in the big, comfy, leather seat. She gazed out the window and saw a house that reminded her of her house in Edinburgh growing up. She felt a wave of nostalgia and was having flashbacks of her early childhood when she first remembered hearing her mother being beaten by her dad.

She looked at her fingernails and despite having nice fancy fake nail extensions on now, she could still remember the days when she had bitten them down so much she barley had any nails left.

She wondered what was in store for her at the party later, maybe she had made a mistake agreeing to this but she could not resist the offer from Simon. He was dressed very sharp, even more so than he normally was. He had a black tuxedo and one of those fancy bow ties and the little handkerchief in the breast pocket. He looked like James Bond and casually smoked a cigar while they drove down the busy carriageway towards Watford. The journey took around thirty-five minutes and they pulled into the country road that led down to the mansion where the party was taking place. Huge trees lined the single-track road on the way up to the mansion. Katie started getting intense shivers and chills down her spine and even jerked slightly at the sensation of it.

"Are you OK, my dear?" asked Simon.

"Yeah," she lied, "I just caught a draft there, I'm fine Simon, are we nearly there yet?"

"Yes, my dear, yes, almost there, try and keep calm. You have nothing to worry about my dear, everything will be fine." He reassured her by touching her right hand, this gave her another wave of shivers and tingles but this time it was more pleasant, she also blushed slightly but Simon did not notice as it was darker inside the black sports car.

Simon parked up beside a row of equally as expensive looking cars. Katie could see Ferraris, Porches, Range Rovers, all the best makes and models of cars you get on the market today. Whoever these people were, they had money to burn, serious money.

"OK, let's go inside Katie, don't say anything to anybody. I will do all the talking, just relax. We will go in and meet a few people then we will get some drinks and a light snack."

"Cool, sounds good," said Katie.

They entered the huge Victorian style mansion; it was like a castle but not quite as run-down. There were hanging plants, hundreds of huge windows, balconies, lots of well-maintained flowers and grass and a little pond in the centre of the front garden area with one of those little angel type statues that had water running out of the penis of the statue. It was really high class and over the top. Katie was thinking to herself, *How did I end up in this kind of place?* She was becoming overwhelmed but put on a calm face.

They went into the mansion. It was stunning, they had huge portrait pictures of old people lined along the halls and lots of antique furniture and artefacts sitting everywhere, deer and other animal heads stuck on the walls, old swords and shotguns on stands and inside very expense looking cabinets. A butler welcomed them in and asked Simon a password before letting them proceed, he leaned over to the butler's ear and whispered something before the butler stepped aside and let them into the main reception area.

The place was very busy. You could see people everywhere stood around chatting and laughing away drinking from champagne flutes. An older man with grey, finely groomed hair and a younger woman, who was around her thirties walked over to Simon and Katie.

"Well hello, young man," said the old chap. "Simon my boy, where on earth have you been hiding?"

"Gregory, my friend," replied Simon. "I have been extremely busy. I was in Milan for a couple of weeks working for Italia Vogue. I would like to introduce you to this very beautiful, young model I have been working with recently, her name is Katie."

Gregory leaned down and took her hand and kissed it like a sophisticated gentleman would do, Katie said, "Very pleased to meet you, Gregory."

Gregory replied, "Katie, you are a stunning young lady, please let me introduce you to my partner Sophia." Sophia gave Katie a quick peck on the cheek followed by a slightly dirty look. She was jealous of Katie due to her looks, this happened all the time, it was like clockwork. Katie and Sophia were probably not going to get along but they kept it civil for the sake of keeping the peace.

Gregory then said to Simon, "So Simon, we have an excellent card of fighters for tonight's event. We managed to source them all the way from Africa, the Middle East and even as far afield as India, our network is expanding at a very rapid rate. I feel you will be most delighted, my dear friend."

Katie paused for a moment and blurted out, "Fighters?"

The others paused, Gregory then said, "Well, yes, the fighters for the blood sport event we place bets on and watch, of course! Did Simon not explain?

Simon interjected and asked Gregory to speak to him in private. They made their way over to the bar and instructed the girls to wait.

They shuffled away and left Katie and Sophia standing together uncomfortably. Simon said to Gregory, "Gregory, my old friend, this girl is a commoner, she would not have attended had I told her exactly what we were doing, she's a damaged one. I have other plans for her involving myself and others in my playroom dungeon, please don't make her nervous, she will make a great victim for us to use up and abuse. Play it calm please old chap, let's get her a drink and put her mind at ease."

Yes, this was the real reason Simon had been courting Katie, what Katie never released was when she told him she ran away from home in Scotland to London and she had no contact with her family or support system down here, he instantly pegged her down as a potential victim for him to abuse in his playroom dungeon, where he and other rich men would carry out sado-masochistic rituals on extremely pretty and younger girls. They were all eighteen or over but not by much and to be honest, sometimes they were a bit a younger. These people were extremely vindictive, they had a strong desire for common girls who would be mesmerised by their money and expensive cars and used these resources to draw them in under the guise that they were just keen photographers looking for pretty models, which was actually true but that was just a smoke screen for the real agenda. These girls would end up being sexually tortured and kept in a dungeon for several days at a time, it was very dark activity. The most bizarre thing is a lot of the girls ended up enjoying it and becoming attached to them, but by that point the novelty had worn off and they moved on to new girls. They got off on the initial fear and this was how they got a kick out of it.

Yes, you could say they were demons, only demons would seek to feed off a human being's fear. Of course, they were human themselves, however deep down, they had very dark and twisted spirits and were most likely possessed. The reason Simon took her to the blood sport event was a simple test for her, if she could accept this, she would be more likely to go along with the next stage of his twisted plan for her. Simon liked to corrupt these girls slowly, he thought of it as putting a frog straight into boiling water – the frog would jump out very quickly if the water was already boiling hot. But if you placed the frog into the cold water first and slowly heated it up and by the time it realised it was in grave danger, it would be too late and the poor frog would be boiled alive before it could jump out the pot again.

Katie was currently in the pot, the water was still only slightly warm at the moment but it was heating up quickly! The two guys went back over to the ladies with more drinks and some caviar and began chatting away, mostly small talk. Katie never mentioned the fighters again, she was scared in case she caused a scene and never wanted to upset Simon and ruin the night so she kept her mouth shut and went along with it. After all, she was in a mansion with rich people drinking and socialising with them. It was a huge step up from her childhood and early period in London, she deluded herself that she had somehow achieved something positive by meeting Simon and being in this situation. How wrong she was.

Around an hour passed and the champagne was flowing like a wild river that had burst its banks and the chemicals were streaming into her brain. This made her feel more at ease and relaxed but she still remained quiet and never said much, neither did Sophia. Deep down they knew they were only there in the first place based on their image alone but that was fine with them. Shallow people need that validation in life to feel worthy; it's a terrible way to live life. Simon was starting to get a bit touchy, feely and flirty with young Katie, which of course made her juices run faster than the champagne! This was calculated and pre-planned, he was now going to make Katie feel like he wanted her in a sexual way and then gradually lower her into his pit of depravity and vile sexual abuse. It was very cold-hearted.

The four of them sat in a lounge/bar area within the mansion mingling with other people at the party. Simon knew a lot of them and they all made an effort to come over and say hello to him and the others. This made him seem more attractive to Katie – Simon was one hundred percent social proof. The type of guy you could take anywhere and his confident aura would charm almost anyone, even the most cautious of thinkers out there. He was good at acting smooth. He was a wolf in sheep's clothing – a man with more faces than the town clock, a deviant, a professional liar.

He leaned over to Katie and whispered to her in his deep husky tone, "Katie, my dear, you look like a princess tonight in that outfit, you know I'm starting to really enjoy your company and I have big plans for you, I'm going to whisk you off to Venice for a few days very soon, we can have a relaxed romantic weekend in the beautiful Italian city. I have good friends there, it will be most delightful, my dear."

"I've always wanted to visit Venice, Simon that would be so nice, thank you."

She was made up by the offer. Did Simon want them to be a couple? She got that feeling; it's easy to get a feeling when you want to feel it to begin with. Maybe he was the one, maybe Simon was going to save her from her life of stripping and prostitution after all, maybe they would end up married and having kids. All these delusional thoughts were racing through Katie's mind right now.

A tall man came into the middle of the room and rang a small bell to obtain everybody's attention and declared, "Ladies and gentlemen, it is time for us to enter the arena! The blood sport event will be commencing very soon. Please finish your refreshments now and make your way to the basement, more refreshments will be made available down there of course. We have all the fighters and the odds at our in-house bookmaker, if any of you would wish to place a wager on any of tonight's fights. Thank you all very much ladies and gentlemen and enjoy the rest of the evening!"

The basement was not like a normal basement in a regular-sized house. It was huge and the entrance to it was a massive metal door, it looked around six feet thick, it was made this way on purpose to drown out the noise. Simon led Katie through the door along with the other guests and there was a makeshift boxing ring type structure in the centre of the huge basement. The guests all wandered in and took seats around the ring, some of them (mostly the males) made their way to the opposite side of the basement where there were little stalls with butlers inside them and these were the bookmakers who took bets on the fights before and during the event. The stakes were high and it was a minimum fifty thousand pounds bet with no upper bet limit. Simon took Katie, while Gregory and Sophia opted to stay seated.

"OK Katie, let's have a look at the fighters."

The butlers had betting slip type cards with all the fights lined up from top to bottom; each fighter had a picture next to them along with their names and their country of origin. Tonight's first fight was between Maria from Argentina and Katja from Ukraine. The girls were victims of human trafficking and were kidnapped in their home countries after being lured into the human trafficking rings under the illusion that they were going to be sent to America or the United Kingdom to be given work and refuge as they were trying to escape their own less fortunate situations. They came from similar dire backgrounds like Katie.

They would be brutally beaten upon kidnapping and if they had children, they would be taken away from them and told they would be used as fighters for the blood sports events that took place all over the world, especially in the United Kingdom, America and Europe. If the woman refused or resisted at all, their children would be executed by having their throats slit in front of them. If they did not have children, their families would be threatened with the same grim outcome if they did not comply. They would also be drugged and raped to instil fear into them and make them easier to control; it was very nasty and cruel activity. Simon never worried about taking new girls to these events if he thought they would make good victims for him at a later date. He had no fear of them being spooked and running to the police.

These events were coordinated by the highest echelons of the global power structure, the top governments of the world and all the organisations below them were collaborating with the human trafficking rings. Who with the networks' agents ran most of the rogue factions of the security services such as the MI5 and the CIA. They had a licence to do whatever they wished and also controlled all the major organised crime in the world. Even if Katie or any other girl were to inform the local police or any kind of authority, it would only go so far up the chain before being nipped in the bud. If anybody kept making any noise about it, they would be very easily disposed of, not that it mattered who would believe a ruffian stripper girl over senior government officials?

Top police chiefs and civil servants were in on this and paid off handsomely by the network to keep their mouths shut and again even if they did somehow develop empathy and decide to speak out, the network via their paid hands within the rogue factions of the spy agencies would either kill them outright or destroy their character and careers via the complaint media who they also owned. Corruption works by getting as many people as possible dirty. The network would routinely get high-ranking politicians and mainstream media moguls drunk and high on mind-altering drugs and then lure them into these situations at these crazy parties at similar type mansions, where they would wake up in a drugged and drunken induced state with underage girls lying in beds with them. They would have secret cameras and audio recording equipment installed in these rooms. This was to ensure all involved would keep quiet or they would be thrown under the bus of public opinion and ruined forever. It was extremely evil and cunning and the saddest part was, it worked extremely well.

Simon placed a one hundred-thousand-pound bet on the girl from the Ukraine named Katja. The odds were 1/1, or 50/50 if you like, even money, which means he would receive 200k, if she won the fight. All the guests were seated and the tall chap who acted as the master of ceremonies stood in the middle of the ring and introduced both the fighters, very similar to an ordinary boxing match. The two girls were dragged out with bags over their heads by big burly bouncer type men and walked into the ring before having the bags removed. It was a bareknuckle boxing/no rules match and they would have to fight until somebody was dead or just stopped moving.

The carrot that was dangled was whoever won would be freed and receive five hundred thousand pounds in prize money and allowed to return to their family. This was a lie. No matter who won or who died during the fight, after it was finished the girl who was still alive would be chauffeured into a small side room in the basement, which was covered in thick plastic sheets. The door would shut behind them and a man would coldly shoot them in the head with a pistol that had a silencer attached to the barrel of it and they would be wrapped up into plastic sheets and tossed into a furnace they had ready. Their ashes would be stuffed into plant fertilizer bags like you see in any garden centre and the groundsmen staff who looked after the gardens and plants at the mansion would use their remains to fertilise the plants and grass. Human ashes were very effective fertilizer and the groundsmen staff had no idea what it really was. They just assumed it was normal fertilizer – of course they did! What else could it be? It was all planned to perfection and it was all very sick indeed. These events were more common than the average person could ever imagine. Or wanted to!

The fight commenced and the girls were beating the hell out of each other, punching, slapping, kicking and scratching. Woman are not built to fight like men, their bodies are not designed for combat. It was extremely grotesque and ugly to watch. Lumps of flesh, skin, blood and hair would get scattered around the ring. The crowd cheer on eagerly as they battled for their lives. Katie was not enjoying this – she was no stranger to violence but this shocked her. However, she played along like a good little demon in training would. She turned a blind eye; she even cheered and pretended to enjoy it along with the other guests. She noticed Simon had a demonic grin and very evil glint in his eye while the fight was taking place. He looked as if he was in some kind of religious trance watching these gorgeous women battering lumps out of each other. He looked sexually aroused and this only turned Katie on more. She felt as if she was starting to fit in with these people. She always thought her dad was the most evil person she would ever meet, but these people were on a whole other level. This was organised evil. She got caught up in the fight and ended up screaming like a lunatic when the Ukrainian girl finally managed to get the better of her opponent. By the time the fight ended, Simon had grabbed her hand and gripped it tightly and they both jumped up and celebrated the victory.

He turned around to Katie and grabbed the back of her head strongly and looked her dead in the eyes and said, "My little lucky charm." He then pulled her towards him and gave her a very passionate and intense kiss. Katie's whole body melted and she felt an overwhelming rush of butterflies racing through her petite body. She fell in love with Simon that very moment. She thought this was the beginning of something really special. It turned out to be only the beginning of the end for her.

Chapter 12

Simon was starting to rub off on Katie, who was now twenty-one years old. They spent a lot more time together since he took her to the blood sport event at the mansion that night. He had now built up her trust and even put her up in one of his swish flats in a much more upmarket area of London. She no longer needed to work at the brothel or as a stripper since he was funding her and giving her lucrative work as a model for several popular fashion magazines and well-known photographers from all over the world. He took her away to European cites on several occasions and showered her with expensive gifts. She was now madly in love with him and was effectively his girlfriend. Of course, he would see other women as well, but Katie was currently the main feature in his rotation. They attended many parties similar to one at the mansion in Watford and Katie grew a chip on her shoulder and developed an elitist ego and mind frame. Some would say she had become more of a snob. Simon had other plans for her, however. He never really cared for her at all; everything he was doing was for his own long-term gain. He enjoyed building girls up then out of nowhere tearing them down and taking complete control of them. This is what made him happy and sexually aroused; power, control and the ability to push buttons to get a reaction. He was a programmer of the female mind and he was a very effective one at that!

Simon was having a drink with one of his hedge fund owner friends that he had not seen for a while but the two of them were close and together they carried out a wide spectrum of sick and twisted games on naïve and pretty young girls in a dungeon, which was located in a safe house they had on the outskirts of west London. It was a derelict old shop they bought over and converted the storeroom into their own little 'play room' as they called it. They were a deadly combination, these two men. Simon was more into mind control and humiliation while his friend who they nicknamed 'Wallpaper Man', he got this nickname based on his facial appearance. His skin was like that old wallpaper people used to have in their houses before paint become more popular. It looked like it was plastered on to his facial bones and sort of matted to his very ugly looking face. He was not an attractive man at all but this only motivated him to become very rich so he could still abuse good-looking women and live a better life. He was short and pudgy and had a very ugly hooked and crooked nose, huge bags under his eyes, which were beady and evil looking, his smile was more of snarl and he actually looked like a gargoyle. He had black greasy hair and was a very sick individual indeed. He was also highly intelligent and made a lot of money through his hedge fund and he was an outright sadist; he was an expert in dishing out physical pain and had a wide variety of torture instruments and countless sexual toys, whips, chains, gags, leashes and the like. He was well tooled up for the task at hand. They sat in the back corner of a quiet London pub one Tuesday afternoon having a catch up.

"Wallpaper Man, my old amigo, how the devil have you been? It's been a while since we spoke in person, what have you been doing with yourself?"

Wallpaper man grinned like a little boy, "I was in Geneva for a few months, I had the most splendid time Simon and I managed to break a few girls during my stay. I had a very kind friend over there who let me use one of his girls for a few days. She ended up having a full-on breakdown, we had to have her killed, she was not much use after that. We heard a few weeks later her father ended up jumping off a bridge because of it."

The two of them laughed in a sadistic manner. Stories like that were very common in these circles, not only did these people ruin other people's entire lives, they left a trail of destruction behind them in doing so. It never bothered them they saw it as collateral damage, not a big deal at all. They routinely destroyed people emotionally, financially and career wise for fun and not just young girls, they would manipulate financial markets, currencies, influence governments, bribe and blackmail businessmen and women for their own self-gain. Lots of people ended up severely damaged or dead due to their activity and it was like water off a duck's back to them. It was like a normal person making a cup of tea – routine stuff.

Simon then said to Wallpaper Man, "I've got a new one in the rotation named Katie – she's a ruffian from Scotland who ran away from her daddy who abused her – perfect meat for us to feast on." (They would sometimes take bites of flesh from these girls during their abuse sessions.)

"Oh really Simon, do tell me more," said a now aroused Wallpaper Man.

"She's very pretty and naïve and never had much in her shitty life, I've put her up in one my flats in the city, she thinks we are a couple and that I love her. She has no idea what I have planned, my dear friend – I'm going to share her with you soon but I don't want to rush this one, I want to build her up slowly then tear her down in a swift and ruthless fashion – you know what I mean, don't you Wallpaper Man?"

Wallpaper Man laughed and said, "Well of course I do, Simon, we are cut from the same cloth, I will be happy to assist you in any way you see fit, my friend."

Simon pulled out some pictures of her that he had taken a few weeks previously and showed Wallpaper Man who made a quiet grunting sound as he eyed up the pictures. "I'm going to make her beg for mercy and cry like a little bitch for us Simon – Wow she is a pretty one indeed, my friend – you never cease to amaze me Simon! My God, you're a dirty, old vile dog! That's why I love you so much!"

Simon patted his back and smiled back at Wallpaper Man, "You know I only keep the best ones for you, Wallpaper Man – I had some others in the pipeline but they were not as suitable and anyways you've been hiding in Geneva recently so I decided to let them go. I took this one to a blood sports event a few months ago – she was shocked but she pretended to enjoy it to appease me! You know those ones, don't you? They know it's wrong but can't resist! My personal favourites!"

Wallpaper Man sniggered and replied, "Yes, Simon, I know the exact type, my friend; those ones always end up being the best victims, you know those ones are a winner! Well done, my dear friend, you're a good soul, Simon, let me buy us another drink." Wallpaper man summoned one of the bar staff over. "Two Glenlivet founders reserve for me and my good friend here. Make them double and on the rocks and make it snappy bar keep!"

Wallpaper Man spoke to people with sheer contempt and arrogance. He really had no respect for everyday people at all; he was an extremely narcissistic character who really valued himself so much higher than other people. He thought he was a good-looking charming man, despite being very ugly and arrogant. All he had was money and the motivation to take advantage of people. He suffered a lot of rejection from girls in his youth before he made his fortunes. He also suffered bullying while he was growing up due to his bad looks. This only made his black heart grow colder over the years and he in effect, just became a bully himself.

It's funny how people who suffer in their early life tend to end up becoming exactly what they hated. It's very ironic.

The two of them sipped away on their scotch malt whisky and chatted about business related issues before Simon declared he must leave as he had meetings to attend in the city later on that day with some shareholders and other clients he worked with. He gave Wallpaper Man a firm handshake and embraced him in an affectionate hug. He promised Wallpaper Man they would be spending time together again soon in the playroom with Katie. Wallpaper Man and him left the bar and went their separate ways for the time being.

Meanwhile, Katie was prancing around her much-improved living environment. Her new flat was really swish compared to the old one she shared with Amanda. They never really kept in touch much these days, the odd phone call or text message was about the only contact they had. Katie never told anybody about what she had been doing with Simon in the recent months. She would see him maybe once or twice per week, unless they had an important photoshoot or some event to attend together.

Katie had been given a crash course in high society etiquette and had developed a new and more proper sounding accent. The time spent around Simon and his ilk had influenced her to become more upmarket and posh. Simon was funding her and she had no work commitments to worry about. She still had a cocaine habit and liked to drink from time to time but it was not as much as previously. She remembered her horrific childhood and the darker days when she first came to London and even ended up homeless at one point and then all the lowlifes and scumbag drug dealers she messed around with. She thought to herself that she had finally achieved something positive in life against all the odds. Sadly, it was all just an illusion, all a big con game that was eventually going to blow up in her face one day.

She now walked and talked with an arrogant aura around her and felt like she had upgraded her position in society, the truth was, she was going downwards not upwards but people are very fickle. Throw some money and fancy stuff at the average person and you shall see the true nature of their character. She was having a bath in her well kitted out bathroom with a large round circular bathtub. She had lots of Yankee candles and nice cosmetics and lots of pleasant smelly stuff around her to create a relaxing atmosphere and she was feeling very chilled and calm as she climbed out the bath and wrapped a towel round her beautiful female body.

She came out the bath and picked up her smartphone, which Simon had bought her. She had an email which was sent to her old email address from her younger years, which she still had active. It was from her old best friend Lucy Smith asking her to call her and she left a mobile phone number to contact her on. Katie was pleasantly surprised. As she had run away, she cut all contact with her family and everybody back home and she had not heard from Lucy for years. She was excited to speak to her and see how she had been doing and also to tell her what she had been up to in London.

Katie got herself all dried and threw on a tracksuit before lighting up a cigarette and phoning Lucy. "Hey it's me Katie, Lucy how are you? Long-time no speak."

"Katie, I know we have not been in touch for years now but I had to contact you, it's not good news either, it's about your mum, do you have a moment to speak?"

"Yeah, sure, what's going on?"

"She's dead, Katie."

Katie froze stone dead. "What do you mean dead? What happened?" Katie was overwhelmed by emotion and could feel tears coming on very quickly. She and her mother had obviously fallen out before she ran away but above all else she was still her mother and still cared about her despite not having the best relationship with her.

"She was found dead a few days ago, I've only just found out, she took an overdose on medication drugs and booze and chocked on her own vomit, your father found her when he came home from work."

"Oh my fucking God," said Katie. "I can't believe this, I can't believe this, what the fuck man!"

"I'm really sorry," said Lucy sympathetically. "I just thought you should know. I hope you're OK. I'm going to leave you now but if you need anything at all and I mean anything, please feel free to give me a call anytime, sweetie."

The phone call ended. Katie paced around in a highly emotional state with floods of memories coming back to her about her childhood, her early years before she witnessed abuse and her mother would hold her in her arms and things were normal to an extent, she then had flashbacks of all the abuse and horrible events that plagued her life afterwards with her sick father and all the twisted games and abuse he would dish out to the pair of them. She wondered if she should go home and see her father but the bridges were already burnt with him, she saw no benefit of going back home and her father never bothered to contact her and inform her that her mother was dead, not that he had any way to do so. Katie had cut all contact and for good reason.

She spent the next few days in a very sad state but after a week or so she managed to pick herself up and was thankful she never stayed in Edinburgh and ended up facing the same fate as her mother. Her life was richer now, she was meant for better things she told herself, she had made it in the big, bright lights of London and was only moving forward not backwards. She grieved for her mother and Simon also helped cheer her up when he heard the news. He was good at comforting Katie and became her rock in life. He was a great listener and he really helped her get over this latest grim news. This only made her bond with him stronger. Simon loved it when he could do this, his control was getting tighter around Katie bit by bit, and she was like a little insect stuck inside the big spider web. Simon was the big spider who had his sight on consuming her mind body and soul. It was done so gradually, like a tiptoe, not too much, not too little. He knew he had Katie so emotionally attached to him now that she was putty in his hands – at his complete and utter disposal. It was now he decided to really move in on her mind. He started slowly becoming more distant with Katie, fewer meetings, less phone calls and less overall contact. This triggered serious alarm bells in Katie's mind. Was he bored of her? Did he have a new chick he preferred? Was he losing interest? Was she not nice enough anymore? None of it was true – he was simply playing a game.

One day, he called her and said he was leaving to go and work in the USA and would not be back for a year, Katie was completely shattered but as it turned out he was just winding her up and told her it was a joke. She was happy he was staying but it was a cruel mind game he was playing. He was just greasing the skids for her to fully submit to him eventually. Katie ended up chasing his validation nonstop and Simon would never give it to her fully.

Yeah sure he gave her a flat and some money here and there and threw her a bone from time to time but she could never get him to fully validate her. This is what kept her around and this is what kept her chasing him ferociously and it kept her in love with him. Katie never wanted to spend time or see anybody else now. Simon was the prize. He was the top of her pyramid and pleasing him was the only way she could be happy deep down inside.

Chapter 13

Wallpaper Man and Simon were out together again. This time they were attending a golfing weekend away in Portugal. They often went away for a weekend or weeklong break together when they both had free time. Simon never told Katie he was going away, he would just disappear from time to time and leave her in London wondering where he was and just as she was on the brink of losing her mind, he would give her a very short text message or phone call just to reassure her he was alive and well and would be back in the city soon. It drove her crazy. She hated it – but also loved it at the same time. Women are very complex creatures and Simon understood this. Wallpaper Man had serious contacts in Europe who were in high positions with the European Central Bank and he had managed to get them an invite to a party that some members of the Portuguese royal family were attending. It was a private and invite only event where several affluent and important people from all across the globe would be attending. Simon was looking forward to this event as he enjoyed expanding his network and huge list of contacts. It pays to know people who have money and power. Wallpaper Man told Simon it would be a great evening for them and they would be wined and dined and then participate in some hunting in the grounds of the castle afterwards. They spent Friday and Saturday playing golf and drinking in the evening with other associates of Wallpaper Man. It had been a long time since they did anything fun together and they were happy to be spending time with each other again.

They were having dinner in a Michelin star restaurant on Saturday evening. A very traditional Portuguese place on the golfing resort they were staying in on the southern coast of the country.

Wallpaper Man was enjoying his fine dinner and said to Simon, "I meant to ask you, Simon, my dear friend. How is this girl from Scotland you were telling me about in London coming along? Katie was her name I'm sure?"

Simon grinned while rubbing his hands together like an evil villain from a cartoon, "Swimmingly, my friend, all going amazingly smooth, she's attached to me beyond repair, I almost have her soul already. Her mother also died recently, so this has helped a great deal."

Wallpaper Man laughed loudly. "Nothing like a good death to enhance the attraction, eh old pal? Ha-ha."

Such a sick-minded chap was Wallpaper Man; he really was a different breed. He was the type of man who would root for the bad guys in movies, loved the idea of a world war breaking out and adored the idea of a violent revolution, which would cause carnage, death and destruction. He was just wired up differently to the average person. This is why Simon loved him so much; he was one of the few people who were actually more twisted and evil than he was.

Wallpaper Man then changed the subject, "This event at the castle we are attending tomorrow, Simon, it's going to be really fun. I don't know if you have ever been to anything like this before, maybe similar but this should be a unique experience for us both. Have you ever been hunting before?"

"Maybe once when I was around twenty-one and visiting Texas, I'm sure I went hunting there for deer one afternoon during my stay. It was very exiting I must admit and I would not mind trying it again to be perfectly frank, old boy."

Wallpaper Man took a small bite of his rare cooked venison steak, chewing away slowly savouring each and every bit of the juicy meat and its wonderful flavour. "This may be a bit different to shooting deer Simon. I mean, don't get me wrong, we are still going to be shooting animals, it's just these ones only have two legs and sometimes talk!"

Simon grinned, "Are you pulling my leg, you twisted swine?"

Wallpaper Man replied quickly, "No, no, I would never do such a thing, old boy, remember this event is being organised by some members of the royal family here, they have the same tastes as you and I, my friend, when it comes to unwinding and having some fun away from our busy and hectic lives. They don't mess around when it comes to a party, I can assure you of that!"

Simon took a big gulp of his red wine. He was eating venison steak also but he preferred it medium rare rather than bloody rare like Wallpaper Man did. "You're some character Wallpaper Man, I remember telling one of the shareholders back in London about your ways, he was in tears with laugher! I really ought to introduce you to him sometime. I feel you two would get along rather well."

Wallpaper Man smiled and resembled what could only be described as a demented penguin. "Please do, old boy, can't have too many friends in this world, I'm sure we would get along and connect well."

They ordered some coffee after their dessert to perk them up a little. Wallpaper Man was chatting away to another associate at the same table about his latest business ventures in Geneva. Simon decided to send Katie a text message to see how she was doing. She replied within a minute, '*Hey babe, I'm fine, just about to have something to eat, hope you're having a great time with your friends. Looking forward to seeing you soon, xxx*'.

Simon and Wallpaper Man paid the tab for the meal and drinks and made their way back to their hotel room. Just as Simon was about to go his own way Wallpaper Man put his hand on his shoulder and said, "Make sure you get a good sleep tonight, old boy, you will require lots of energy for tomorrow evening. Call me when you're up and we will make the final arrangements, I will have a driver collect us from here and bring us back afterwards."

Simon nodded his head in agreement and said, "OK, my friend, have a good sleep and I will see you tomorrow."

They went their own ways and had an early night in preparation for the private party tomorrow at the nearby royal castle.

Simon and Wallpaper Man were collected from their hotel in a very swish looking Jaguar sports car. It was all black paint with blacked out windows. The royal family provided all the transport for the guests who were attending the party. The car pulled up to the castle, Simon was impressed.

"Wow look at this fine piece of architecture," said Simon to a clearly excited Wallpaper Man. The castle was pristine and the gardens were absolutely immaculate and very well maintained. There was very lush looking grass and countless beautiful plants and ornaments scattered around the vast grounds. Simon was used to visiting nice places but this was something else.

Wallpaper Man turned around to Simon and said with an eager tone, "OK, old boy, let's make our way into the castle reception area. We need to book in and register our presence before we can carry on with the proceedings, I'm so glad we are attending this event, old boy. I'm confident you will enjoy this evening and leave with fond new memories." The two of them made their way to the castle reception.

The décor inside was really fancy and expensive looking; it was fit for a royal family indeed. A butler welcomed the two of them and they made their way over to a big, shiny desk to sign in. Wallpaper Man spoke Portuguese fluently and the staff member behind the desk appreciated his efforts for using his native language. They were booked in and allocated seat numbers for the six-course dinner they were having; this was to be followed by some speeches from special guests and members of the royal family before the hunt was to take place in the early evening. The meal was exquisite as expected and two old friends had some great chat and conversations with some other guests who were at the same table. One Swiss banker was trying to convince Simon to invest vast amounts of money into the crypto currencies named Bitcoin and Litecoin. Simon had some basic knowledge of these new markets but was not currently invested in it. The Swiss banker named Pierre managed to convince him to dump some money into his Bitcoin derivatives trading company, which he assured him would be a worthwhile investment in the future as the big global bankers plan to eradicate conventional money and make a crypto digital currency the main world currency in the future, so it was wise now to invest into this market while the price was still relatively cheap and easy to get involved with. Simon committed to invest around two hundred and fifty thousand pounds for starters which pleased Pierre. They exchanged contact details.

The speeches after the meal were rather interesting and one member of the royal family was given a standing ovation after his lengthy diatribe about the state of the world and how the global elite have to implement new modern techniques to regain control of the public psyche. The rise of the internet and independent media had thrown a spanner in the works as the plebs had now grown distrustful of the mainstream media, which they control and they had to introduce more internet censorship and new hate speech laws to combat the rise of undesirable information being available to the masses. The Silicon Valley companies who own all the major social media platforms were all in on this and had agreed with the global elites to assist them in their latest campaign to censor their platforms using advanced algorithms to filter out any prominent independent voices being heard and more importantly repeated by the masses. It was all very organised and all major world governments were in cahoots and willing to assist the overall effort with stricter censorship laws and allowing mass immigration from the Middle East and Africa to demoralise and destabilise the western nations via terrorists attacks and cultural change. This would distract the indigenous populations' attention away from the global elites' masterplan and far right figures who were on the payroll of the elites would play a key role in winding up the masses into an anti-immigration frenzy. It was all orchestrated with great insight and forward planning to bring about their end goal – a one world government, one world currency and one world military. A high-tech surveillance world police state, which would require total compliance from the masses or they would have their ability to purchase food removed via the world crypto digital currency. The key advantage to not having physical money is the ability to simply cut any dissident's cash flow away if they spoke out against the system and they would starve to death. If not, the militarised police force would simply arrest them for a made-up hate crime and they would be thrown into a prison camp to be 're-educated'. If they showed the notion to then comply, they would be let off but the majority of them would be tortured to death and disposed of. It was a hellish plan but these sick and twisted elites had a disdain for humanity and would stop at nothing to achieve this heinous and wicked plan for the world. Simon and Wallpaper Man were aware of the plan but were not involved at the highest levels but they supported it in spirit and also shared the same contempt for the average person. They viewed them as victims; pawns to be used and abused. It was a superiority complex ingrained into the minds of these types of people. The scary part was that their plan was real and was being rolled out slowly as each year passed. It was only a matter of time before it was fully implemented.

All the guests were invited to the hunt, which was taking place from a high balcony on the rear end of the castle overlooking a vast forest that went as far as the eye could see. They were provided with loaded shotguns and some spare ammunition. The prey was not deer or any other animal, which you would associate with a conventional hunt, it was mostly children which had been kidnapped ranging from the ages of ten upwards, both male and female. The high-level elites were deeply involved in rancid paedophilia activity and ran huge child sex slave rings across the globe. It was the biggest secret in world history that the vast majority of people in society never knew about. It was a really dark and vile world. Simon was into some pretty sick stuff but even guys like him had some morals and would draw the line at the really nasty and vindictive stuff but the royal elite bloodlines and the top banker families went that step further. They were on a whole another level. They used this activity not only for their own sick and demented pleasure, they used it to control high-level government people.

Back in the 1950s being gay or accused of being gay was enough to blackmail anybody into submission but in these modern times that was no longer enough. It had to be a bigger taboo, had to be more shameful so they used child abuse to control the top tier people who were in the public domain; leaders of nations, top media moguls, prominent celebrities with large followings. It was a perfect set up for the elite. To get into these high positions, you had to take part in these bizarre satanic child abuse rituals to become part of the club and be allowed to operate. If you did not wish to comply, your career would all of a sudden come to an abrupt end. If you decided to make a noise about it, you would be shamed in the public domain and or sometimes just killed off. They would say it was suicide, drug over dose or some terrible freak car accident. This is why you often hear of well-known singers, actors and the like suddenly dying and these reasons are provided to the public as an explanation. The vast majority are murdered in cold blood for not being cool with this stuff and are then seen as a threat and executed by the paid hands in the intelligence and security services or highly paid ex-mafia or organised crime hitmen who will kill anybody provided the price is right. It's extremely common. What they do to these children who are mostly from care homes or born into this lifestyle by willing collaborators is quite frankly beyond the pale. It's much deeper than basic sexual abuse, it's based on satanic practices and they go to severe lengths to terrify these children into pure submission. Once they are used up, they are often killed or released back into society as mind-controlled damaged vassals who end up going on to become abusers themselves. This is why child sex abuse cases are always on the increase because there is a steady supply of future predators being dripped into the mainstream of society. Many of them are programmed then placed into shadow government departments where they become kidnap ring coordinators and end up becoming exactly what they hated. It's all very creepy underhanded activity.

Wallpaper Man had the shotgun up against his shoulder as he was perched over the edge of the huge balcony alongside the other guests, who were taking shots at the live targets.

He said very loudly, "Keep running little boy – you can run but you cannot hide, peasant!" *BANG, BANG, BANG.* He let off three shotgun blasts and the poor boy's body blew into several pieces and blood spattered everywhere, he was only around three hundred or so yards away and the shotgun shells ripped his flesh and bones apart.

Wallpaper Man took a big puff of his cigar and said, "That was a fine fucking shot don't you agree, Simon old boy? That little rat was zig-zagging his run to try and avoid my torrent of bullets, but you need to be extra quick to avoid the infamous sharpshooter, Wallpaper Man!" He gave himself a pat on the back as the other guests laughed at his crude statements. Wallpaper Man was involved deeply with the child kidnapping rings. A victim of abuse himself by his dad and uncles, he was the perfect man to run such a programme, he had zero empathy and ran his black operation kidnap squad like a military unit. He actually enjoyed doing it, it was a like a hobby to him even though the high-level elites he supplied with kids paid him handsomely for his work.

This is also the reason he was able to gain lucrative government funded contracts and was made savvy to insider information regarding the stock market and the world economy. He was really dirty and ruthless and his kidnapping teams were always the lowest of the low scum. He employed middle-eastern and eastern European mafia thugs who would do anything for money to do the dirty work but he ran the operation with swift precision. Simon was aware of this but always turned a blind eye, he knew Wallpaper Man was a deeply sick individual but never wanted to be involved with it directly like he was but he understood it did go on at the higher levels.

Simon and Wallpaper Man continued hunting the child victims who were being released from the castle dungeon and desperately tried to run to safety but most of them were mowed down by a hail of bullets before they could get away.

Sure some of them managed to avoid being shot but there were security guards and big Doberman attack trained dogs all around the perimeter of the castle who would take care of any of the poor kids who made it that far. They would either be shot in the head or ripped to pieces by the aggressive Dobermans who roamed the grounds looking for prey.

After some post hunt refreshments, Wallpaper Man asked Simon if he wished to attend the torture dungeon in the castle with some of the royal family and other elites but he declined and said he was too tired and had a very early flight to catch back to London, the following morning. He promised Wallpaper Man he would join in next time round and told him to make contact with him when he was back in the UK, so they could abuse Katie together as planned.

Wallpaper Man said, "I should be back over there in a few weeks or so, old boy – I would not miss it for the world. Thank you for coming, Simon. I really enjoyed spending some quality bonding time with you again and I look forward to ruining that dumb jock cunt with you soon in our playroom. Safe journey back to Britain, old boy."

Simon went back to the hotel and left the following morning for his 8 a.m. flight back to London.

Chapter 14

Meanwhile back in London, Simon was getting ready to get Katie into the playroom with him and Wallpaper Man. Katie was more delusional than ever and was under the impression Simon was going to propose to her any day now and they would become a married couple and ride off into the sunset and live happily ever after. Oh how wrong she was!

The two of them were having a chat in the flat she was staying in. "How did you get on in Portugal, darling, was it fun? Bet the weather was better than over here! Was your friend Wallpaper Man happy to see you, sweetie?" Simon nodded his head in agreement.

"Yes it was marvellous, Katie, speaking of Wallpaper Man, I showed him some photographs of you and he is most eager to meet you. I spoke very highly of you, Katie. He should be back over in London in a few weeks. We should have a get together."

"Yeah of course, darling. Sounds great," replied Katie.

Simon then got on to the topic of rough S&M sex. Simon and Katie had been having a lot of sex recently and he was quite rough and dominant by nature but he wanted to test the water with her by taking it a step further.

"Nothing too extreme, darling, just some ropes, gags maybe a bit of whipping, nothing to worry about at all – all good fun. Would you be up for some more kinky fun with me?"

Katie blushed slightly. "It actually makes me quite horny; the thought of you doing that stuff to me, babe. You're a great lover as it stands but I would most definitely be up for doing some kinky and filthy things with you."

Simon grinned slightly and quickly pulled Katie close to him and said in a very deep and sexy tone, "That's a good girl."

Katie's heart melted, she was so in love with Simon, at this point she would have found it hard not to do anything he requested.

"I have a play dungeon in West London. It's all kitted out with everything we need to have some real good fun. I'm going to take you there soon and we can experiment with each other. It's something I always try and make time for. Don't worry if at any point it becomes too much, we can stop and have a break." Of course Simon was lying. He had no intentions of having 'kinky' sex with Katie in the playroom. He was simply just luring her in so he and Wallpaper Man could have their wicked way with her. Afterwards he was not bothered how this would affect her or what she would do. If she freaked out and ran away fine, if she became more attached and more into him that was also fine. It did not matter to him because as soon he was done with her, he was going to cut her loose regardless, as he had no further requirement of her and would move on to his next target. He never usually bothered with the girls afterwards.

Once Simon had completed his original mission, he usually became very bored of these girls and tossed them to the side of the road like damned dogs with zero empathy; not a care in the world. Sometimes he kept the girls around but not often and if he did, it was strictly as abuse victims (he called them 'pain pigs'). He would never take them out again or give them anything other than another vile session in the playroom. He had done this several times before and he was keen to ruin Katie once and for all and ditch her, with the help of his trusty friend, Wallpaper Man of course, who was still currently in Europe dealing with several other business-related issues and of course, his other twisted endeavours.

"The guys are starting to get annoyed, boss. They are looking for more money for these new no bid contract jobs you are getting from the Saudis, it's not as easy anymore with everybody now having smart phones with HD cameras on them, it's more risky so the guys are looking for a pay increase to match up with the heightened risk factor."

Wallpaper Man was having a meeting with his head supervisor Ivan. Ivan always called him 'boss' and he was a good skivvy for Wallpaper Man. He was the most senior one in Wallpaper Man's kidnap squad and did a decent job keeping the goons in line. He was trying to negotiate a pay increase for the other men in his crew. It was not going very well, thus far. Wallpaper Man did not like to be asked to pay more money or do any favours. He was a taker – not a giver.

Wallpaper Man was sitting in his main office with Ivan. Ivan was a huge, intimidating figure with a very muscular build and short trimmed, military style hair. He looked like a nightclub bouncer. Him and his squad of around eight thugs would roam the streets day and night and kidnap unsuspecting kids from random streets, play parks, playing fields and school playgrounds. Anywhere at all really, they had no issues just taking a poor kid away forever, to be sold into sex slavery by Wallpaper Man to very rich elites. Sometimes they would be provided with specific targets by Wallpaper Man and they would stalk the kid and the kids' family and work out their daily routine of all the members so they could decide the best time to snatch the kid undetected. They even grabbed kids from peoples' very own backyards, while they were taking the trash out to the rubbish bins outside. They were real sick lowlife scum, the type of guys who would sell their own mothers for a quick buck. No empathy, no morals, no sense of decency. They had several successful missions under their belts and made Wallpaper Man very large sums of money over the years.

The meeting continued – Wallpaper Man took a small sip of his scotch and looked Ivan up and down before slamming his fist down on the desk and launching into a frenzied verbal attack. "ALL THESE FUCKING YEARS, I SHOWED YOU AND THE OTHERS NOTHING BUT LOYALTY! AT ANY POINT, I COULD HAVE FUCKING BURNED YOU ALL, HAD YOU ALL LOCKED UP, THROWN TO THE EAGERLY AWAITING WOLVES! YOU WANNA GO

DOWN FOR BEING A KIDDY SNATCHER, IVAN? EH?
COULD YOU IMAGINE BEING SENT TO PRISON FOR
THAT? BIG FUCKING TOUGH GUY!"

Ivan was trying not to flinch, despite his size and build he was scared to death of Wallpaper Man, he knew exactly what the evil little demon was capable of and he knew for a fact he would not hesitate to dispose of him and have him arrested for his part in the operation in a heartbeat. That's the thing about this vile and dark activity, once you get involved, it's very hard to get out of it. The dark controllers know this and make sure everybody involved is dirty and compromised, so they are always of use to people like Wallpaper Man and they can always do the dirty work and ensure the elites have a nice steady supply of kids for their demonic pleasure. It's extremely organised. If only the public knew about this. If only.

"No disrespect meant, boss, I'm just passing on the message for the other guys. I'm very happy with the payments, sir, I promise."

Wallpaper Man sat down and had another sip of his fine scotch malt whisky, he composed himself and calmed down a bit then said, "You're a good boy, Ivan, you know that right? I would never have anybody else from that crew you run in your position, you have the stature, the brains and most importantly the experience to keep running these operations – you're a key member of my team and I need you to remain focused on the task at hand. The Saudis have a very specific taste and I have some key targets for you to track down and capture over the next few months so I need you to be strong, level-headed and make sure we don't fuck this up because these Saudis pay top dollar and do not take kindly to being let down. I'm going to give you and the guys a pay increase at the end of this year, as I've agreed a higher wholesale price with all of our clients. Please relax, son. You're in good hands."

Wallpaper Man stood up and walked across his huge desk to Ivan and directed him to the door while he had his hand around his back in a kind of father and son bonding moment.

As they walked toward the door, Wallpaper Man patted Ivan's back and said, "Thank you, Ivan. I will be in touch soon, try and chill out for now and inform your crew I will increase the fee at the end of the year, it's only a few months away, but for now the price is fifty thousand per unit."

"OK sir, thank you for your time, boss, have a great day."

Ivan left and Wallpaper Man closed the door firmly behind him before making his way to his desk.

Wallpaper man placed his backside on his huge leather seat and took a deep breath and smiled with a sick grin. He thought to himself, *How dare that pleb even have the audacity to demand more money from me. He is getting too confident.* He opened his laptop and contemplated contacting the police chief, who was on his payroll to go and arrest Ivan for his insulting remarks. Wallpaper Man was extremely greedy, very disloyal and he would not think twice about stabbing somebody in the back, if he felt for one second they were not dancing to his tune or playing his game the way he wanted them to. This is why he was so rich and powerful, he had no empathy for people. Even the most subservient loyal minions like Ivan were always at risk of being tossed away, he had done this with several associates over the years. Even his close ally and confidant Simon was not safe and he almost had him killed over an old business deal that went sour on Wallpaper Man's end, but he decided against it as in the long term it may well have hurt his own interests down the line. He had super human levels of insight and intelligence. His IQ was so high he had to attend a special college in Norway to sit the exam because the online test he had done could not register his score. He was the definition of an evil genius and his lack of morals just added to the sinister nature of his character.

He sparked up a fine Cuban cigar, stood up and walked towards the huge black mirror he had in his office. Black mirrors are extremely uncommon as they don't give a good reflection due to their colour but evil people like Wallpaper Man had them in every single one of his offices or residences. It was a spiritual mirror that Wallpaper Man believed channelled dark energy from the underworld and gave him more power. Of course, it was all hocus pocus bullshit but these guys don't always operate within logic. He was very involved in occultist practices and often he would sit alone and do Ouija board rituals and interface with spirits and demons and they gave him information and guided him to make certain decisions. When most people sit alone and think, their thoughts are normally innocent and mild for the most part but when Wallpaper Man does this, he can hear screaming and grotesque spirits calling on him and pushing him to on carry out his demonic activity.

He was tormented to the core of his black soul. He often joked with fellow elites about how he is worried about dying because he does not want to face up to what he has done in the afterlife. He prayed every single night for life extension technology to be invented so he could live forever in his spiral of self-gratification and bathe in the filthy pool of depravity forever. His worst fear was dying and being forgiven to be sent to heaven. He wanted to reside in hell, the devil's realm where he could rule over the weak sprits and reign supreme for eternity. Despite being very intelligent he did have flaws and was seriously delusional at times but he always remained focused on his own interests, first and foremost. He was very tight fisted with money, he would often argue with restaurant and bar staff about petty bill disputes and he would constantly complain to companies and raise grievances just to get a small financial reward. Everything was just an ego-based contest to this man. He would disagree with everybody not because he had a valid point or actually cared, he just liked to win the battle regardless of the end result or the original aim. This is why he excelled in business negations because he would just bore or frustrate people into agreeing with him. A flawed genius would be an accurate description. A deranged psychopath who was in tune with the all the dark energy the spiritual underworld had to offer.

Chapter 15

Simon and Katie were getting kinky in the bedroom. Simon in his slick wisdom was greasing Katie up for the hard-core torture session with himself and the sadistic Wallpaper Man. However, he knew the best plan of attack would be to gradually ease her into the whole S&M bondage type sex beforehand, so when it came to the 'playroom' session, she would be comfortable as she would have had plenty of experience beforehand.

The two of them were in one of Simon's houses having some filthy fun. Katie was suspended from the ceiling in rope bondage while Simon was walking around her in a circle with a large whip in his hand.

"You are my property now, bitch, do you understand?"

Katie replied, "Yes, sir." She was becoming very well trained and more obedient to her master, Simon. It was so intense and erotic she was not really interested in normal sex anymore, it never gave her the rush she was craving and she just found it terribly boring and mundane. This was the way forward for her now.

The session continued – "I'm going to administer some pain now, slut, I know you enjoy it because you're a damaged messed up piece of shit." He whipped her hard across the breasts and she screamed in pain. The sound of her physical pain made Simon aroused and he continued to whip her for a while longer while she was still suspended from the ceiling.

Her body had lots of marks left on it from the whipping and she was extremely aroused from it. He untied the bondage ropes and gave her a very subtle kiss on the forehead and said, "You know you're my favourite girl in the whole wide world, don't you babe?"

Katie had a mini breakdown and began to cry. The reason she burst into tears was the overwhelming range of emotions she had just experienced then with Simon showing her some cute affection straight afterwards, she simply could not cope. Simon knew exactly what he was doing, this was one of his strategies, get the emotions in turmoil, engage her full range of complex female emotions in a short space of time to send her into a frenzy. It was all a big mind game to harness control over Katie.

Simon spent the next few hours fucking Katie very rough while she was restrained with her hands behind her back tied together. She was in the doggy style position. He was giving her vile verbal abuse at the same time and she climaxed on several occasions during the steamy session. Katie was in ecstasy and enjoying every moment as she screamed in sheer pleasure and delight. He was like a wild animal rutting a female mate and was very vocal himself during the whole time they were having sex.

"Who do your holes belong to, bitch?" he shouted at Katie.

"Yours master, they're all yours, defile me, make me your fucking slut," she screamed back, as Simon pounded her very hard and fast until he himself came to a long awaited climax and let off a huge grunt and squirted his fertile man seed deep inside her soaking wet vagina. Simon did not worry about Katie getting pregnant as he made sure she was taking the pill every day to ensure she wouldn't. Katie hated the pill as it gave some her side effects she could have done without but she worried if she stopped taking it, Simon would not want to have sex with her so she took the pain to appease him. Love will make people do crazy things after all.

After the rough and passionate session, they lay together in bed and held each other and both of them felt very relaxed and content with life. Katie drifted off into a sleep whilst still in Simon's arms. After a few hours, they both surfaced again and Simon got up and declared he had to get ready for a meeting he had to attend in the city that afternoon. Katie was sad that he had to leave but understood his work was important. He took her back to her flat and headed into the city for the meeting.

Simon entered the boardroom to attend the meeting with the shareholders, the top executives and big wigs of a bank he worked for. They were discussing how to save money and wanted to axe some of the senior management figures who currently worked for the bank. Simon had earmarked one guy named Alistair Mckendrick, who was a ruthless director but had been overstepping the mark in recent years with his heavy-handed approach towards the staff who reported to him.

Simon opened the meeting and said, "OK guys, Mckendrick has to go, I'm not happy with his attitude and I don't think he is the right person to take us forward, he is too old school for this day and age and every manager below him is now gunning for him, awaiting his demise, he made some low level supervisor cry the other day for something really petty, we don't need somebody like him anymore."

One of the shareholders then said: "He used to be really good to begin with, always met his targets, God knows what's happened."

Simon replied, "We get this issue quite often, these guys become too arrogant and big for their boots, the petty piece of power they have goes to their feeble minds and they then become out of control and start throwing their weight around like lunatics. End result, the whole workforce becomes less productive and in the long term we lose profits and end up with a high turnover of mid-level management because they can't work with them any longer. Two of them have already left this year and I managed to contact one of them and he told me the reason was because Mckendrick was putting him under too much pressure, which he felt was unjustified. I never spoke to the other one but I would bet the reason he left was the same."

Another shareholder piped up, "Well Simon, we know the problem, the question is, what is the solution? Mr Mckendrick has been with the bank for around 25 years now, how do we get rid of him without excessive funds being spent to pay him off? He will be due quite a bit of compensation I would imagine. Is there anything we can do here to avoid this?"

Simon replied, "I think the best way forward is a restructure, we will shift Mckendrick into a mickey mouse role and put in that new young gun who is working for him currently – what's his name again that small chap from up north I believe, Scott Flannigan, he would be better for us now, I think. We will tell Mckendrick's current staff to report to Flannigan now and inform Mckendrick he no longer has any staff to worry about, this way he can't annoy anybody expect us, maybe, in fact that synergy project crap would be a good one for him to take on, let's make him project manager of that busted flush and hopefully this will bore him into leaving rather than paying the idiot any severance money."

Simon took a sip of water and got the nod of approval from the board members and shareholders. "Good idea, Simon, see how that goes and hopefully saves us a bit of pain." Simon then asked if there were any more pressing issues to address before he could leave the meeting. He was excused and made his way out the boardroom, another successful meeting under his belt.

Simon was a good businessman, he knew how to get people on board and come to a mutually beneficial agreement, nothing like Wallpaper Man, who was a corporate bully type that would never bend for anybody. If he was tasked to get rid of Mckendrick he would have set him up to be sacked rather than shuffle him out the way quietly. He was just a different animal altogether. He had no room for compromise, it was his way or the highway. It's a double-edged sword. It works well but you become hated in the process by your staff below you. This did not bother Wallpaper Man in the slightest, he actually preferred being hated. The bad energy and vibe fed his dark soul better than any love or admiration ever would. To him, hate was love.

Simon went home and decided to contact Wallpaper Man for a chat. Wallpaper Man quickly picked up the call from his office in Geneva.

"Well hello, old boy, how the devil are you, Simon? What grants me the pleasure of your fine chat today, my good friend of old?"

Simon laughed a little and said, "Wallpaper Man, I come with good news dear pal, she is ready now."

Wallpaper Man made a creepy grunting type sound and said, "Oh really now old boy, how delightful, that's wonderful news, is she now primed and prepped for our playroom session, the dirty little swine?"

Simon laughed again, Wallpaper Man always made him smile he had such a sarcastic and evil tone to his voice it was hard not to find it amusing, he really was like a sick, evil villain from some movie or comic book.

Simon replied, "Yes, my friend, she is ready to rock n roll, I have introduced her to all that silly bondage stuff, you know the drill, these girls love that crap, the filthy little animals they are, she can't get enough. We will be able to do our thing to her without too much hassle, I would imagine. When are you available to fly over?"

Wallpaper Man made yet another seedy sound and then replied, "I can be in the UK by Friday morning, old boy."

It was currently Tuesday afternoon.

"Friday, OK, sounds good to me, let's have the session on Saturday evening, that will give you time to get a good night's sleep after the flight. You know what the rigmarole of airports and travelling is like these days, what do you say to that, old boy?"

Wallpaper Man took puff of a cigar before saying, "Saturday Evening is great, old boy; that suits me to a tee, Simon. I will have my PA book me a flight and hotel room immediately!"

Simon ended the call and was relieved it was finally arranged. He was looking forward to showing Katie the meaning of 'true love' as he called it. This session was going to be extreme for her, think kinky S&M sex times ten million. It was proper hard-core and nasty sadistic stuff. He could not wait! And he knew the sick bastard Wallpaper Man would be more than game for it as this type of thing was his forte. Simon decided to go for a bite to eat with another friend in the city of London and planned to inform Katie of his plans the next day. The whole time Simon had been interacting and spending time with her was in preparation for this. It was all planned out from the day she made the mistake of meeting Simon for the photoshoot.

Chapter 16

"I love being your kinky, little slut, babe. I would do anything for you Simon, I love you with all my heart," Katie was out with Simon at a trendy bar in London for a few afternoon gins. Simon had been telling her about his 'playroom' and Katie was excited to visit and have some fun with Simon there. She had no clue about Wallpaper Man's attendance. Simon planned to keep that to himself to increase the shock factor. Once she was there and tied up, Wallpaper Man would appear from a side room with a creepy Halloween mask on. He loved wearing scary masks to terrify people. Also, he was so ugly the mask looked just as bad as him, if not slightly better. But the fear element was the main reason he wore such masks during these types of sessions.

Katie and Simon were chatting away while sipping some really expensive and strong gin. Simon said to Katie, "Oh yeah, I meant to mention this to you, the editor of a very prominent fashion magazine contacted me in regards to yourself darling, he wants you to model for them in the next couple of months, first in Milan then Paris and also over in New York. You will be busy for a while but you will be paid handsomely for the work. I can join you in Europe but I may not be able to make the New York part of the trip. (None of this was true, he was just making up stories to keep her happy.) Katie smiled like an innocent, little school girl, her gorgeous face looked amazing when she smiled in that manner. She was such a stunning looking woman.

"Wow, babe," she grabbed Simon's hand, "you're so good to me, baby, I'm so happy I met you, all these opportunities and work you have provided for me, it's been amazing being with you, you have changed my life for the better. Thank you."

Simon gave her a kiss on the forehead and told her, "It's my pleasure, sweetie, you're going to repay me soon at the playroom, aren't you?"

Katie blushed and looked right into his eyes with her freaky, little glare in those big, pretty blue eyes, "Of course, master, I would do anything for you – and I mean anything."

Simon gave her a deep passionate kiss.

They had a few more drinks in the bar and then decided to make their way over to the west end for some food. They were not a great distance from the restaurant they were going to eat at so they proceeded by foot. As they were walking along a busy London street, they heard a large crowd up ahead in what appeared to be a protest of some sort. Thousands of people with yellow hi-vis vests on where stood with big signs, placards and a leader type figure from the protestor group with a megaphone was giving a speech to the crowd in front of him.

Katie and Simon had to walk around them all and overheard the man with the megaphone speaking. He said very passionately, "The people are awake, the people are sick and tired of our cowardly political class selling us out to their globalist masters, we are sick of the megabanks running our country, running our government policy and most importantly running our lives!" The crowd cheered him on. "No more will these traitors be allowed a free reign. No more will they continue to sell us down the river to hell. We must stand up to these scumbags, we must let them know where the true power is, we must remind them, we are the people and we ultimately dictate the direction of our country, they are in office to serve us, not themselves, not their paymasters at Goldman Sachs – us – the people!" The crowd cheered again.

Simon and Katie made their way past them all into the distance out of earshot. Simon was visibly angry. Katie asked him what the matter was.

"Did you not hear that fucking animal? The plebs are starting to get wise now, these are sad times we live in Katie, they are becoming very angry at this system, the one we thought we had built to perfection to serve us – the elites. I'm getting a tad worried – I hope our plan to dissolve these movements is deployed in full soon or it won't end well for people like me."

Katie at this point had a grasp of what Simon meant but was not really aware of the bigger picture. She knew Simon and fellow elites had a plan for the world and saw themselves as superior to the average person, but she was herself just a working class runaway who was blessed with good looks and enough charm to get her up the ladder slightly.

She calmed Simon down before they made their way into the expensive looking eatery in London's upmarket west end. After some lovely food, Katie asked Simon why he was so annoyed at the protestors they walked past earlier that evening. "It's just not a good sign for us Katie, everything we have done in the past throughout history has only been successful because it was done in the darkness, the people were never meant to find out about who really runs the world, the media used to give us all the cover we needed but these days things have changed. The rise of the internet and twenty-four-hour information available to all has allowed a lot of people to become far more aware of our operations now. Therefore, it's a lot more risky and a lot harder to get away with certain things. We need to be hidden, hidden in plain view, if that makes sense. *Prima Facia* is the Latin phrase for that. It means it's so obvious but you cannot see it. Now it's still as obvious as ever but more and more people, everyday normal people can get an insight into the bigger picture. It's highly concerning but I am confident we shall prevail in the end."

Katie asked, "Why do you need to be so secretive about it all?"

Simon looked down to the ground then slowly raised his head, his eyes did something extremely freaky and weird looking, his pupils went huge as if he was on drugs and he looked at her with a stern stare and said, "Little people don't deserve to know the truth, they are not capable of understanding the complexities of it all, they are not worthy of the knowledge that me and others like me possess. We are much better equipped to decide the direction of the world and the whole human race, not them. It's always been this way and in my view, it should always stay that way or else the rabble will ruin everything, this is something that may be totally incomprehensible to you and to be brutally honest, I would expect it to be. You're a working class girl from the poor council estates of Edinburgh but thankfully you are a beautiful looking girl and we can connect on many levels but on this profound subject, I'm afraid, it may be just a bit out of your capabilities to grasp it fully or get behind it like I can."

Katie replied, "I want to help you and become a part of it Simon, I hate working class people now. I grew up around them and I see the basic mind-set and their lack of intelligence and basic world view, you have helped me understand that the higher echelons of society are the better areas to be active and involved in."

Simon grinned, "You're a good girl, Katie, but please, just relax and enjoy the ride, you don't need to be concerning yourself with this just now. You are doing great with the modelling work and being my main girlfriend. I'm happy with your contribution, so just look pretty for me and keep doing what you're doing, my darling."

Katie nodded with a cute smile on her face. As long she could keep him happy, she was happy. She enjoyed serving Simon, she enjoyed being submissive to him in every way not just sexually. It was very fulfilling for her. If only she knew what this twisted man was really doing with her long term. It was so vindictive, so cruel and so evil. It would not be long before she realised exactly what the 'bigger picture' for her was going to be! They say the road to hell is filled with good intentions!

Saturday arrived. Tonight was the night Katie was eventually going to enter the playroom and be broken by the love of her life, Simon, and the crazed psychopath Wallpaper Man. It was a very dark grey and horrible night in London. Which was quite a coincidence considering how Katie's evening would end up turning out.

Simon was in one of his penthouse suites with Wallpaper Man making the final preparations. Wallpaper Man was sharpening one of his torture instruments that he had acquired in London earlier that day. He was sat in front of a huge mirror stroking the medieval looking device with some kind of sharpening stone tool. "I tell you something, old boy, this girl of yours is really in for a treat tonight. I just found out this morning that I lost a considerable amount of money in a botched heroin wholesale deal in Albania, I'm really fucking pissed off and I'm going to need to have some people in my network executed for letting me down in this perverse manner."

Wallpaper Man was up to his eyeballs in narcotic dealing. He was a wholesale merchant of just about every illegal drug you could buy. He loved the fact the puppet riddled governments kept all the drugs illegal to insure the price and therefore profits remained a lot higher and guys like him could make a tasty profit and of course have anybody involved who stepped out of line, arrested and sent to jail for lengthy periods and or killed like he was planning to do to whoever had fucked him over in this failed deal in Albania.

He shipped heroin in bulk from the far and Middle East and had it smuggled through his trafficking networks, which operated with impunity. They just paid off senior customs officials and had a free reign to ship in as much as they wanted into mainland Europe, the UK and the USA.

This latest deal had gone sour however, turns out an Albanian mafia faction decided to rob it as they were not aware of who was behind the huge shipment of grade A pure heroin from Afghanistan. They managed to hi-jack the shipment and Wallpaper Man was certain somebody from his network had leaked information to the rogue mafia gang allowing them to pinch the shipment and get away with it.

He was planning to interrogate Ivan and a few of the other senior members of his crew who were in-charge of this operation. He knew one of them was responsible. Not Ivan himself but somebody Ivan had delegated the running of this particular shipment to.

Ivan was in trouble for allowing it to happen and would have to come up with answers and give at least two names of potential suspects for Wallpaper Man to investigate. It was not going to be a fun meeting that's for sure.

Wallpaper Man was more angry than normal due to this robbery, so Katie was in for some real horrible and excruciating pain tonight.

Simon walked over to Wallpaper Man and tried to reassure him, "These things are always bound to happen with the narcotics smuggling, old boy, I did warn you about this a few years ago when you took this work on, but don't get yourself in a state over it. In our line of work, you always get people on your side that want to leave the plantation and make themselves a quick buck at the expense of the greater good."

Wallpaper Man shook his head slightly, "I remember your concerns, Simon old boy, maybe I should have listened but the money was too good to turn down. Plus I enjoy the fact the drugs I smuggle around the globe are wreaking havoc on people's lives and getting them into trouble with the local police forces. It's actually more rewarding than making money from it. Every time I hear of some peasant drug dealer being busted and thrown in jail or some heroin addict overdosing, I smile inside knowing I probably contributed to their downfall. I get off on seeing others fail more than I do being successful myself! I crave others to be damned with misery, pain and failure. It is my soul food, my mental nourishment and my passion."

Simon burst out laughing and said, "Dear God, old boy, you really are a different breed, I mean, we are all evil bastards and we know it of course, but you! You, my oldest and dearest pal, you are a special type of sick, it's legendary how you perceive the world and go about your dealings, when you die, God forbid anytime soon, I will make sure we have a statue and shrine of your good self somewhere for us all to remember the notorious Wallpaper Man. In fact, let's have a drink now, old boy, let me get you a malt whisky, I know you love a scotch, old boy!" Simon made his way over to his swish looking drinks cabinet and proceeded to pour his dear friend a large scotch on the rocks.

Wallpaper Man always had his whisky on ice. He never used a mixer, he hated watering down his drinks as he loved the sharpness and bitterness it would create on his diseased tongue. It summed up his character to be honest, raw and uncompromising. The two of them sat down and continued to drink and chat for a while before getting themselves ready to head to the playroom. Simon was going to drop Wallpaper Man off at the playroom then go and collect Katie and return to the playroom for the session. She thought the two of them were just going to have some extra kinky fun that night like they had been doing before and she agreed to put a blindfold on before they entered the playroom to add to the 'excitement' as Simon sold it to her. Silly woman never had a chance.

Wallpaper Man was in the playroom alone awaiting Simon and Katie coming back. He was pacing around like a lunatic. He often did this before he engaged in depraved sexual acts or before an important business deal. People like Wallpaper Man with a very high IQ score tend to be like this and walk around in circles bouncing off the walls. It's because they have so much going on inside their heads that they can't sit still and relax for long, especially before key events in their life.

He had all his toys and instruments ready and of course, his extremely creepy looking Halloween mask that he had with him for the session. It was like a demonic clown mask with big scars and boils all over it. He thought it was beautiful. One time in France, he was being taken to some elite event at a castle in Normandy and he noticed a dead cow on the side of the country road that he and his driver were travelling along. The cow had been dead for a good while and it was rotting away with maggots eating away at its horrible looking carcass. Wallpaper Man ordered the driver to stop so he could look at it more closely. He stood outside the car and stared at the disgusting sight for nearly thirty minutes while slightly drooling saliva and making very weird grunting and almost sexual like noises. This is what this sick freak found nice to look at. Most people admire a good view of a mountain range or a blue lake on a summer's day with nature and everything else living happily in harmony but this kind of beautiful scene to Wallpaper Man was ugly. He preferred the sight of death and failure. He actually had artwork all over one of his properties in Europe of children being slaughtered and chemical weapons being rained down on innocent families with troops in dark outfits oppressing them. He found this macabre stuff a work of art. You could simply not get as twisted and sick as this character was. He was deranged beyond repair. He was looking forward to this playroom session tonight, however, and he decided to take a moment to try and compose himself before Simon and Katie arrived.

He took a seat in the far-left corner of the playroom and had a crystal glass with a single malt scotch on the small table next to the black leather seat. A voice came into his head and said with a demonic and evil tone, "My sweet child, how you have served me well, how you have honoured my sprit with your fine work over the years. Keep feeding me, my sweet child. Keep up your good work. But always remember, my child, always remember that I know everything about you and I'm never going to leave you." Wallpaper Man felt shivers racing up his spine and had to jump again and distract himself for a while. That was extremely profound, he thought. He was used to interfacing with demons and sprits but this time it really hit home and had a chilling effect on him. What did it mean by 'I know everything about you and I'm never going to leave you'? Was he being watched at all times? It sounded that way. He downed his scotch whisky in one huge gulp.

He poured himself another drink and took a big sip and pulled a grin when he felt the sharp liquor slither down his throat and into his belly creating a warm fuzzy feeling before the chemicals entered his bloodstream and made him feel slightly drunk. He took another seat and sparked one of his fine Cuban cigars and said to himself, "I'm going to destroy and defile this bitch tonight, I'm going to show her the meaning of pain." He grinned to himself for a moment while puffing his expensive cigar.

The playroom was extremely well-for the task at hand. It had everything they needed to perform their deeds on the naïve young girls they would lure in. The room was quite small but was all very neat and tidy and laid out well. It had a dungeon type of vibe, very dark and harsh looking. There were chains and ropes laid around the perimeter of the room and they also had a cage which sat in the far-right corner. It was big enough for a human to get into but only if they were on their knees. They would put girls in it for days and feed them via dog bowl. It was a humiliation tactic that they used. They also had an electric chair type device, which they would strap victims into before pulling a lever which was attached to the chair and came out from the side of it. It had three different settings. The first setting was just a very mild electric shock which could be left on for any length of time without doing any real harm to the victims other than a sharp tingle. The next setting was a much higher voltage that would be discharged into the victim's body. It was still not enough to kill anybody but would be excruciatingly painful. The third and final setting was enough to kill somebody if left on for more than ten seconds. The pain this would create would cause the victims to lose consciousness in most cases and they would be left in so much pain they would never really be the same again and one girl they had in it previously ended up foaming at the mouth due to the shock it created within the body. It was like a mini lightning bolt. The device was built by a sadistic engineer that Wallpaper Man knew in Germany. Simon flew him over and had him build it for them in the playroom a few years beforehand. They used it on most of the victims they took back there and it was their favourite torture device.

There was also a CD player and speakers connected to it which sat on stands in the room on which they would play very scary and creepy music during the sessions. The only way you could describe it was a combination between terror music from a horror movie crossed with boiler room type music. It also had demonic screeches, which played randomly throughout the session to instil more fear into the victims. Not that they weren't terrified enough to begin with!

Simon and Katie were in his car on route to the vile playroom. Katie was a bit nervous but also excited at the same time and she said to Simon, "I can't wait to see the playroom and what you're going to do to me tonight. I must admit I'm really horny."

Simon glanced over at her and smiled, "Oh don't you worry, babe, I'm sure we will have a great time. It's about time you had a session in the playroom with me. Only my favourite girls get an invite to this special place of mine."

Katie blushed slightly and thought to herself, *he must really love me now to be taking me there.* The car was cruising along a section of the motorway and the traffic was pretty quiet in this part of London for a change.

After another ten or so minutes of driving, they arrived at the playroom. Simon parked the car up behind the old building that led into the playroom and said to Katie, "OK sweetie, that's us here now, step outside the car and walk towards that blue door over there to your left. I will get the blindfold from my suitcase." Katie stepped out the car and walked towards the door slowly and stopped. Simon came up behind her and leaned over to her left ear and said in very sinister and vindictive tone, "Now you're going to learn what I'm really into, tonight you're going to see how nasty and vile I can be, bitch." Katie felt a rush of butterflies race up from her belly straight into her naïve young mind. Her heart was racing, pumping blood around her body at light speed. She was now extremely nervous but she trusted Simon at this point. She was guided into the playroom, and strapped down to the electric chair and the blindfold was removed. The first thing she saw was Wallpaper Man stood over her with the creepy clown mask on. She screamed in horror at him then the scary music kicked in and her heart sank. She knew then she had made a drastic mistake. Alarm bells were ringing and she was now at the mercy of two absolute lunatics.

Katie was released from the playroom around three days later. She could not remember how long exactly she was in for but she was tortured and abused in very sick and sadistic ways. She had been drugged, physically attacked, raped, humiliated, whipped, belted, canned and suspended upside down for hours on end. She experienced severe mental and physical trauma and was now a broken person in a delusional state. She almost forgot who she was and during the time in the playroom, she experienced horrific flashbacks of her abuse from her father back home in her younger years. Wallpaper Man even put on a Scottish accent at one point and pretended to be her father while she was under the influence of the cocktail of drugs they injected into her veins. She was in a horrible state with huge scars all over her body and big bruises covered the majority of it that were not cut, she even had teeth marks in her stomach from where Wallpaper Man had bitten huge chunks out of her skin like a possessed vampire.

Simon had taken away her keys to the flat he was allowing her to stay in and she was once again homeless. She ended up in a women's refuge shelter with nothing. No money, no job, she was robbed of absolutely everything. Simon had disappeared and was now out of contact.

She thought about contacting the police but was too afraid as she knew Simon was connected and nothing would happen to him. She also never wanted to get him into trouble because a big part of her still loved him despite the abuse she suffered that night. One night in the women's refuge centre, she attempted to take her life by hanging herself with some bedsheets in a disgusting, unclean shower but a volunteer who worked there managed to grab her just before she carried out the fatal act. She was very angry at the woman for doing this as she was so depressed and confused, she saw no other option other than to end her miserable life. But sadly for her, she had to carry on for the time being. She had learned a very harsh lesson and was now faced with a big dilemma in life. What was she going to do? How was she going to survive in this cruel world with no job, no friends, no money and nowhere to go? She could have went down the honest path now but the thought of going out and working a mundane job of utter drudgery was of no interest to her after living the high life for so long with Simon and not having to graft away for a living. She had to use her only real asset which she still had intact – her good looks. She was now twenty-five years old and still had her natural beauty. And it was going to come in handy very soon.

Simon and Wallpaper Man just carried on as normal. Events like this were nothing to them, it was just another day at the office to these guys. Wallpaper Man spent some more time in the UK with Simon before heading back over to Europe to deal with the informant in his smuggling network, who cost him a large amount of money by allowing a huge shipment of heroin to be hijacked. It was not going to end well for this informant and Wallpaper Man would soon also face retribution for countless crimes against several people.

The bad guys do run the world, this is a fact. But every now and again even the callous and most ruthless face karma for their disgusting actions. Wallpaper Man had started to really annoy some very rich and powerful people that even he could not out-spend or stop and he was going to face the wrath of the larger criminal network for his long list of reckless actions and mistreatment of people across the board. The hierarchy had a price put on his head and he was soon to be dealt with in a very cold and heartless fashion. It was to be a fitting end to his crime and depravity ridden life. The orders were clear. It was not to be quick, it was not too be pretty and he was going to be made an example of to send out a strong message to all the people in the network from the top tier controllers all the way down to the goons doing the dirty work on the street level.

Wallpaper Man was interrogating the suspected informant with Ivan in his office in central Geneva. His name was Paddy. He was a low-level, half-Irish, half-American hoodlum who was part of Ivan's crew. The interrogation was not going well for any of them. Wallpaper Man had Paddy tied down to a chair and was questioning him, "So Paddy, we have three options here, boy. Number one is you admit to being a thief and tell me where the shipment is and I will let you off with minimum punishment. Number two is you tell me who you're working for and where the shipment is and I will also issue a lenient punishment in return. Or you maintain the lie, you don't know where it is and I will torture you to death. What's it going to be Paddy?"

Paddy was shaking and replied, "I swear, boss, I don't know where it is. Please believe me, I swear on my mother's life."

Wallpaper Man sighed deeply and launched into a crazy tirade, "YOU DON'T FUCKING KNOW? LIES PADDY! FUCKING LIES!" he pulled a cut throat razor from his jacket pocket and sliced it down Paddy's left cheek as he screamed in sheer agony, the blood was gushing from the deep open wound and Wallpaper Man laughed and said, "OK, let's start again Paddy. WHERE IS MY FUCKING HERION, YOU THEIVING, IRISH, GYPSY CUNT? TELL ME RIGHT NOW OR I'M GOING TO CARVE YOU UP LIKE A FUCKING TURKEY!"

Paddy was now in a terrible state of panic, he was stuttering and said, "Please, please, Wallpaper Man, I had nothing to do with this, I swear I don't know."

Wallpaper Man shook his head and sat down and remained silent for a brief moment before looking up at Ivan and giving him a slight nod. Ivan pulled a small pistol out of his hip holster and put a bullet straight through Paddy's head in a cold-blooded execution like style. Wallpaper Man was not even in the mood to torture Paddy. He knew Paddy was clueless about the shipment but decided to have him murdered regardless. He had done this to many innocent people over the years.

Wallpaper Man sighed again and said to Ivan, "Get rid of that waste of space now." Ivan delayed for a brief second then Wallpaper Man raised his voice and said, "GO ON IVAN, GET THAT FUCKING THING OUT MY OFFICE, YOU USELESS CUNT!"

Ivan sprang into action and quickly dragged poor Paddy's now lifeless body out of the office to be disposed of out the back entrance. Like many others before, Paddy was discarded like leftovers from dinner. Wallpaper Man knew now he was in serious trouble. The elites who he was working for were very dangerous and connected people and they were putting serious pressure on him to find this shipment. He had no solid leads on how it was hijacked and knew if he never came up with answers soon, he would be in grave danger himself.

A few days later, an agent who worked for the De Johor family (the people who Wallpaper Man ran the drug and kidnap rings for mainly) contacted Wallpaper Man. Initially, he was worried when the call came through but the agent assured him that they had found the shipment via their own means and were contacting Wallpaper Man with good news and in good faith.

They wanted to offer him a promotion within the network as they were impressed with his work despite the minor issue with the heroin shipment being lost temporarily. Wallpaper Man was so made up and excited that he never realised he was walking into a dire trap. Power hungry maniacs can sometimes become very gullible. They instructed him to attend a palace they owned in the Netherlands the following week and Wallpaper Man was like a little boy who was eagerly looking forward to Christmas day.

He picked out his best and most expensive suit and even had his hair done all nice and neat and made sure he looked his very best despite being very ugly regardless. He was flown to Amsterdam then collected at the airport and transported to the Palace for the meeting. He was being offered a higher tier position within the network, which would allow him to make much larger sums of money and it would also allow him to remove himself from the more front line, blue-collar element of the elite network activity. He would also be granted diplomatic immunity and it would become more or less impossible for him to be arrested regardless of his crimes. He would be issued with new special privileges and enter the core leadership of the network and be invited to the very selective and inclusive meetings, events and parties that previously he was not welcome to attend. It was a dream situation for Wallpaper Man. He was buzzing at the mere thought of it.

He made his way into the huge palace and was greeted by friendly staff and led into a meeting room that the family's agents and some more senior members of the actual De Johor family were sitting inside waiting for him. There were four huge six-foot-six plus security guard types stood around the door outside the meeting room. Wallpaper Man walked past them and he entered the room and bowed in front of the De Johor's like a star struck fan boy meeting his favourite celebrities. They were extremely rich and powerful, so he felt he had to show them respect. Winston De Johor (the second-in-command of the family headed up by Baron Dennis De Johor) told him to take a seat in front of the round table, which the family and their aides were sitting at.

Winston said to him, "Mr Wallpaper Man, what a pleasure it is to have to have you here. We are all glad you are present and well for this initiation into our inner circle. Congratulations, sir. We are going to go through a few details first before we head down the stairs for a celebration and of course, the final part of the ritual."

Wallpaper Man was so happy, he really was on cloud nine right now, they chatted away about his new special privileges and new businesses he would be in control of and all the good stuff that came along with being part of the inner circle.

They then made their way down the stairs to another room, which sat below the rear end of the meeting room. On the way downstairs, Winston said to him, "Ah, Wallpaper Man my boy, this brings back memories of my own initiation many moons ago, it's a wonderful day, enjoy it!"

As they entered the large room, Wallpaper Man noticed something very strange in the centre of the room. It was a huge fish tank with what looked like six piranhas inside who were all swimming around in circles very quickly. Next thing, one of the big security guards smashed a baton clean off the back of Wallpaper Man's ugly, little head. He was knocked out cold. A short time later, he woke up and the first thing he could notice was a strong smell of what could only be described as a pâté or meat paste of some sort. The guards had smeared it all over his body while he was out cold. He was then brutally beaten by the four security guards with their batons while sobbing and crying for his daddy. They say when people are facing death, they cry for the people they love the most. Even evil demons like Wallpaper Man would often do this, when they know they are close to the end. He was then strapped into a cage still conscious and lowered into the tank of the ravenous piranhas. The cage door was opened via a remote control that one of the guards had and the viscous and predatory fish proceeded to rip his body to bits for around thirty seconds or so taking huge chunks of flesh out of his torso and legs in the process.

He was then hoisted back out of the tank and slammed down on the floor still semi-alive and conscious covered in his own blood, bones and guts screaming like a banshee in terrible agony and pain just like the many victims he had inflicted similar pain on before. They left him there to bleed out for about an hour until he eventually died. A fitting end to the vile excuse of a life he lived.

The De Johor's never found out where their shipment of heroin went and since Wallpaper Man never had any answers and could not locate it, they assumed he had stolen it so he could keep the full profit for his own greedy pockets. They also were aware of all the reckless stuff he was doing and the whole network was getting sick of his notorious over-the-top actions as he was attracting too much unwanted attention. They had a sit down with all the heads of the network beforehand and after some discussions the hit on him was approved. They lured him into the meeting in the twisted manner in which they did because like Wallpaper Man, they were all evil and sadistic bastards and wanted to teach him and any others a lesson and terrify the whole network and all the associates involved within it to show them that they would face a similar fate if they themselves stepped out of line. The whole event with the piranhas in that palace was filmed and the footage was sent around the network via their private email server on the dark web under the subject title 'Consider this a warning shot over your heads!' They even sent it to Wallpapers Man's dad who was very elderly and in a critical condition inside a hospital in Geneva. The rumour is he was so shocked and upset he took a massive heart attack and died on the spot. Simon also received the footage and it shocked him to the core of his soul. He thought Wallpaper Man was untouchable. Turns out he was not. He ended up suffering depression and had to take a lengthy time away from all his business dealings and other activities. Nobody had seen him for months and he lost a lot of money because of this. There was a rumour he took his own life after a large drug overdose but this was not confirmed.

There is no honour amongst thieves and no matter how bad or tough one thinks they can be, there is always a limit. Always a bigger and more ruthless enemy, who will pop up out of nowhere and take you out regardless of your reputation. Wallpaper Man learned this the hard way. As did many others before him and many others would find out after him in the seedy echelons of high society.

Chapter 17

Katie managed to move to back to Scotland after a few months in the refuge centre. Her old friend Lucy Smith was currently single after breaking up with her long-term partner David Power and she was living in a flat in the Leith area of the city with her young two-year-old son, Brandon. Katie contacted her via email as she had lost her mobile phone number during her hectic time in London. She told Lucy what had happened to her and she felt very sympathetic and promised not to tell anybody as it was a sensitive subject and Katie was ashamed of herself for letting it happen to her in the first place. She did, however, revert back to stripping again and was working in a run-down club in Edinburgh full of losers and stag parties, not anything like the high rollers she got accustomed to in London in the previous years but it was better than working a low paid job in a more moral line of work. She never made much money but it was enough to give Lucy some for letting her stay at her flat temporarily. She knew she could not stay forever and had to somehow find a way to be able to move out comfortably.

The two girls were sitting in the flat and young baby Brandon was playing with his toys. Katie was getting broody looking at the kid and she was craving a child of her own.

She said to Lucy, "Aww he is so cute and gorgeous," turning towards the confused child, "who's a handsome boy? Come here and give Auntie Katie a cuddle." Brandon burst out crying in a panic and desperately leaned towards his mother. They say children can pick up on vibes from people and if this was the case then Katie certainly did not give off a good vibe!

After what she had done in London, it was not a surprise either. Her soul was most likely corrupted, possibly doomed to hell forever. Once you dance with the devil, you must be sure you really wish to do so because that one dance may well last you forever! Katie was now paying the price for her bad life choices but considering how her childhood had went, she was really up against all odds of having a happy and peaceful life. Maybe she craved a hectic existence, maybe she enjoyed turmoil more than security. She certainly felt that way in the past but was now starting to adopt the view that maybe she would be better off settling for a more quiet life with a nicer type of man rather than rich, dominant, alpha males, who would only use and abuse her as she had previously found out first-hand.

Either way, her life was a lot less uneventful now. She never had the vast funds that were made available to her in London with Simon and all the modelling work she was able to do via his contacts. She thought often about Simon and everything he said to her about life and she now had a much wider worldview and obtained key insights into how the elite class of society thinks and how they see the world and the average person.

Katie and Lucy decided to head out for the evening as Brandon was being looked after by his father. It was a mild weathered Thursday night in Edinburgh and they were inside a run-down pub in Leith. The girls sat in the corner of the bar having a few drinks but nothing too major. They chatted away and looked at their mobile phones from time to time and Katie was looking around at the people in the pub. She was thinking about the day she met Simon at that fancy Italian place in Belgravia and how much more classy and expensive it was and how good he looked in that Gucci turtleneck and how stunning she looked that day as she was trying hard to impress him. She missed Simon a great deal. Of course, she hated him for the lies he had fed her and how he led her on for so long and made her feel as if things were going to advance in their relationship, only to lure her to that horrid playroom and do all those disgusting things to her with his wicked friend

Wallpaper Man. She never saw Wallpaper Man's real face during the vile occasion and it was probably not a bad thing considering how ugly he was but she still got chills in her spine thinking about that creepy mask and all the cruel stuff they did to her. The scars on her body mostly healed or faded away but the mental ones were never going to go away. They would haunt her forever.

Lucy went up to the bar and some greasy rough looking man tried to chat to her but she quickly dismissed him as he was very drunk and not very attractive. She went back to the table with the drinks and Katie was sitting staring into space reminiscing about her life and how she ended up living on her friend's couch back in Edinburgh after everything that happened. Was this really what the plan for her life was? Was this why she went and did everything she done in London. Just to come back here and sit in this slightly damp, smelling cheap working class pub with the average plebs? She was not exactly in a happy place but understood her trip to London was a lot of fun to begin with but things quickly turned sour. From the scumbags and lowlifes who fucked her around to meeting Simon and the elites. It seemed to be all in vain. But she decided from now, she was not going to dwell on it and stop chasing after pipe dreams and find herself a good man to settle down with.

She wanted to get married and have kids one day with Simon but this was clearly not meant to be, so her new aim was do it with somebody else. Somebody a little more stable, somebody who would appreciate her and be a good husband and father. She needed something different. Women never know what they want deep down but at a certain point in their life, they tend to stop going after the bad guys and look for more gentle natured men. This is what she planned to do now. Find a good man who was happy with her lifestyle choices and make a go of it with him and see how it went. If he was suitable, she would be looking to have kids and settle down with him. The question was now – who would the lucky chap be?

The girls had a quiet night and went home semi-early. Katie was very sad and depressed again because she was feeling lonely and unwanted. She needed a new man in her life and decided to try out a popular dating app to see if she could meet anybody nice. Being as attractive as she was, this did not take her very long. She had a date lined up with a guy named Steve and he agreed to meet her at a local coffee shop the following day for a casual chat. He was a decent looking guy with short brown hair, not very tall but taller than Katie but not as hot as Simon or some of the geezers in London she was involved with previously and he seemed nice on the several messages they exchanged beforehand.

Katie arrived at the coffee shop and Steve was already there. She was actually around twenty minutes late but Steve never said anything to her. This was his first mistake as Katie automatically saw him as weak for not having a backbone to at least ask her why she was so late. He was extremely nice and bought her a few cups of coffee while they chatted. He complimented her nonstop and kept telling her how beautiful she was and how wonderful it was to be in her company. Katie thought too herself, *this guy is perfect. He is already obsessed with me. He could make a good boyfriend.* He was one hundred percent cool with her stripping occupation and was he was just glad to be on her good side and being able to spend time with her.

They had a few more dates over the next few weeks and Steve always paid. He was not rich but had a decent enough job and never complained about paying for all the meals and drinks. He was being played but his craving for love and affection from a beautiful woman clouded his logical judgement. He was nothing like Simon or any of the other men Katie had become accustomed to over the years. Their romance flourished and Steve became madly in love with Katie and constantly contacted her and wanted to spend more time with her. He was overwhelmed by her beauty. It's safe to say Katie became annoyed with him and his obsession over her but this was exactly where she wanted him at this point in her life. This would be the man she would settle down with and end up bearing children with.

Over the next few years, they continued to go out and became an official couple. They moved into a small house together on the outskirts of Edinburgh. One day, Steve was coming home from his work, (he worked for an insurance company and it was a white-collar cubicle job) which was stressful and not very rewarding. He had no passion in life other than Katie and she knew this. Over time, it actually disgusted her how attached he had become to her and she knew if she ever did leave him he would be lost. Completely lost and would have no direction in life. She felt more pity for him than anything, she even made him grow a beard to try and make him more manly looking as he was always cleaned shaved. He hated the feeling of the hair on his face and he thought it made him look scruffy and unclean but he did it anyway to appease her. This of course just made her hate him that little bit more. He entered the house and Katie was in the bedroom upstairs still asleep after being out all night to silly o'clock partying with some friends she worked with in the strip club. Steve made his way into the kitchen to get himself a drink and a light snack and noticed the kitchen was rather unclean and messy so he started to tidy it up a little.

Katie came down the stairs and saw what he was doing and said, "Do you think I'm here just to clean a fucking kitchen for you?"

Steve turned around confused and said, "No sweetie, not at all, I just thought I would tidy it up a little before I made myself a drink and a small snack." Katie just sighed and walk right past him into the living room. Steve followed her in like a puppy dog trying to appease its annoyed owner, "What's the matter, darling?" he asked.

"Nothing," replied Katie in a cold tone.

She was in a bad mood today and decided poor Steve was going to face the brunt of it. She was a damaged woman from her past and every now and again she would have very bad mood swings and give poor Steve grief for nothing. The naïve and love struck fool would always assume he had done something wrong to deserve it and desperately pander to try and appease her again. She would snap out of the mood eventually but sooner or later, she would start her nonsense again and Steve would be at the mercy of her random outbursts. He took a lot of verbal abuse from her and she would belittle him and questioned him as to why he did not earn more money and mock him because he always got shafted at work and had to work late quite often.

Katie was not really attracted to him at all anymore but she still stayed with him for the security. They ended up getting married and went on a cheap skate honeymoon to Spain. Katie was very ungrateful and awkward the whole trip and she often longed to return to her days in London with Simon prancing around the fancy bars and restaurants eating and drinking the best quality products with the upmarket people. She missed the high life a lot and was always sad that she was tossed away in such a cruel manner by Simon. Her resentment, however, was always aimed at Steve. It was a sad situation for him.

She cheated on him from time to time with clients from the strip club who were attractive. They were always tall, bad boy, alpha male types but nothing like Simon's level, just run of the mill dudes who wanted some fun with a hot chick. Steve never found out and never wanted to find out either, he was a complete and utter cuck of the highest order. They had a huge fall out not long after the honeymoon and he cried like a silly little girl. Katie just pitied him but she stuck with him for the safety factor and the fact she wanted an obedient man to have kids with as she was sure some alpha male guy would leave her a single mother and once again depressed and lonely only with a child or two to look after. This is what Katie, the blue-eyed girl, who went beyond what her mind was really capable of was trying to avoid her whole life. It's a shame she had to settle for something less than she actually craved deep down but this could be said about a lot of woman.

When a woman gets married, the white dress is meant to symbolise purity. In older times, a man would not marry a woman unless she was a virgin. This was no longer the case –

right or wrong. She had managed somehow to escape a horrible childhood and gained a lot of unique experiences during her time in London mingling with the elites and being able to spend a lot of money without a care in the world. She had grown older and wiser but was eternally damaged from her past and this would never change.

One sunny day in July, Katie gave birth to a beautiful baby girl. She was sure it was Steve's but she had been cheating on him a lot before she found out she was pregnant, so she was not one hundred percent sure of this. Steve only got sex once every two weeks or so, if he pandered enough and Katie could bring herself to pretend she enjoyed sex with him as he was useless in bed and never showed nearly enough dominance or aggression. She did miss some of the kinky sex she partook in during her glory days in London but was not as bothered about it these days as she was older and felt she had got most of it out of her system now.

She named her new baby daughter Hallie and the feeling she got when she gave birth and became a mother for the first time was the happiest Katie had ever been in her mostly sad and miserable life. The unconditional love and admiration she had for that little girl filled her damaged heart and soul with nothing but pure joy and fulfilment. The bond she felt was so strong and it really did change her life for the better. Steve was a great dad to this child despite the fact she may not have been his and he also loved the little girl with all his heart. He managed to get a promotion at work and was earning more money now. Katie gave up the stripping and became a full time mother and she began to study at night classes as Steve's parents lived nearby and they were more than happy to help out looking after their first-born grandchild. She chose criminology as her main subject and found it very interesting and she already had a lot of experience with street level and very high-level criminals. She hoped one day to do a master's degree on the subject but she was just happy to be doing something productive with her life for a change.

One night after her night class was finished, she was waiting in the car park for Steve to pick her up and go home.

Her phone rang and she assumed it was Steve but the number was from an international code. She had no idea who it was, probably a cold caller from a marketing company or a wrong number maybe. It was a cold caller, just not the one she expected.

"Hello," she said.

"Hello Katie, how are you, my dear? Have you missed me?"

Her heart sank and butterflies flew around her belly at the speed of a thousand gazelles – it was Simon!